The Joy of Noh

The Joy of Noh

*Embodied Learning and
Discipline in Urban Japan*

KATRINA L. MOORE

SUNY
PRESS

Cover image: © Katrina L. Moore

Published by State University of New York Press, Albany

© 2014 State University of New York

For information, contact State University of New York Press, Albany, NY
www.sunypress.edu

Production by Jenn Bennett
Marketing by Anne M. Valentine

Library of Congress Cataloging-in-Publication Data

Moore, Katrina L.
   The joy of noh : embodied learning and discipline in urban Japan / Katrina
L. Moore.
      pages cm
   Includes bibliographical references and index.
   ISBN 978-1-4384-5059-9 (hardcover : alk. paper)
   ISBN 978-1-4384-5060-5 (pbk. : alk. paper)
   1. Noh.   2. Women in the theater—Japan.   3. Women—Japan—Social
conditions.   4. Acting—Study and teaching—Japan.   I. Title.

   PN2924.5.N6M57 2014
   792.082—dc23   2013019517

10 9 8 7 6 5 4 3 2 1

To my parents, Atsuko and Ian Roger Moore

Contents

List of Illustrations

Acknowledgments

Writing a book incurs many debts. I would like to express my profound thanks to the many people who supported me as I conducted my field research and wrote this book.

As an ethnographer, I rely on the willingness of people to share their lives with me. I owe my greatest debt to the people in Japan who allowed me to become a part of their lives. I would like to say a special word of appreciation to Kobayashi Sayu, Koei Hoshino, Miki Yukiko, Nishii Aya, Tada Yoshiko and Tada Kunio, and Tsutsumi Yumiko and Tsutsumi Yoshihiko. I thank each of them for giving so generously of their time and for opening many doors that facilitated the development of this research.

At Harvard University, I was fortunate to have on my doctoral committee Theodore C. Bestor, Helen Hardacre, and Arthur Kleinman. I thank them for their unwavering support in all aspects of my work, and for critical comments and encouragement to take my work in new and challenging directions. Theodore C. Bestor's ability to keep a finger on multiple threads of investigation, along with his strong commitment to ethnography, has inspired my work. I owe profound thanks to Helen Hardacre for her intellectual guidance and sustained moral support throughout my years of graduate school. She continues to be an inspiration and role model. My sincere gratitude goes to Arthur Kleinman, whose generosity as a mentor and keen analytical insights have been invaluable.

My colleagues at the University of New South Wales have been generous with their time and insights. I wish to thank especially Tanya Jakimow, Paul Jones, Amanda Kearney, Vicki Kirby, Andrew Metcalfe, Michael Pusey, Louise Ravelli, Claudia Tazreiter, Carla Treloar, Melanie White, Marc Williams, and Mary Zournazi. I have also discussed some of these ideas in seminars at the University of New South Wales. Students in my seminars at the University of New South Wales offered engaging and thought-provoking feedback. Their insights and responses to the seminars have helped to inspire the writing of this book.

I wish to thank various friends and colleagues who provided inspiration and support during the writing of this book: Vickey Bestor, Holi Birman, Margaret Bruce, Manduhai Buyandelger, Ruth Campbell, John-Daniel Encel, Alisa Freedman, Junko Maria Furugori, Marilyn Goodrich, Zahra Jamal, Vera Mackie, Bakirathi Mani, Priscilla Song, Helen Snively, Rebecca Suter, Sarah Wagner, Allison Alexy, Joshua Dasey, Ivan Goldberg, Sue Hilditch, Lindsey Morse, Ursula Rao, and Sarah Teasley.

I would like to acknowledge the generous research support of the following: the Japan Foundation, Wenner-Gren Foundation for Anthropological Research, Reischauer Institute of Japanese Studies at Harvard University, Cora Dubois Fund, and the University of New South Wales Research Promotion Grant. Sections of chapter 4 of this book appeared in the following journal article: "Transforming Identities through Dance: Amateur Noh Performers' Immersion in Educational Leisure" *Japanese Studies* 33, no. 3 (2013): 263–277. For permission to publish photographs of Noh performances, I gratefully acknowledge Kobayashi Kan who has made photographs available for this book.

I would like to thank Nancy Ellegate at the State University of New York Press for her enthusiastic support and sage advice in the revision of this manuscript, and Jenn Bennett for her expert help in preparing the manuscript for production.

I am very grateful to the reviewers of the original manuscript for their insightful comments and many constructive suggestions.

I thank my family for their love and affection. I would like to express my deep and enduring gratitude to my parents, Atsuko and Ian Roger Moore, for their love and support. To my sister, Lisa Moore, I thank her for her patience and good humor. Finally, my deepest gratitude goes to the women of the Sumire Kai who welcomed me into their lives and entrusted their stories with me.

Note to Reader

Japanese names are given in this book in the way they are used in Japan, with the family name first.

Macrons are used throughout to mark long vowels in Japanese, with the exception of well-known places such as Tokyo.

Monetary values are provided in yen. The exchange rate has fluctuated during the period in which the fieldwork for this book was conducted. For the purpose of comparison, however, in October 2013 one U.S. dollar was equivalent to 103 Japanese yen.

Introduction

One evening I attended a dinner party in a French restaurant in Tokyo. I sat next to a physician, Sakurai Fumiko, who talked enthusiastically about her passion for singing the lieder of Franz Schubert. Fumiko had begun taking singing lessons in her mid-fifties in a private class. As she spoke of these lessons she seemed to be divulging a special dimension of herself that was still something of a secret but becoming an important part of the way she defined herself.

Fumiko introduced me to her friend Yamada Miki, who had just turned sixty-seven and had similarly begun a new learning pursuit when she had entered her late fifties. Miki's learning was tai chi. She began it, she claimed, to pave the way for her "second life" (*dai ni no jinsei*). Now, more than ten years into her tai chi passion, she was a licensed teacher of tai chi at a "silver university" in which the majority of her students were in their sixties and seventies.

As my circles of research contacts grew, I realized that Sakurai Fumiko and Yamada Miki were part of a vast and dynamic public culture of later life learning in Tokyo. I discovered that many women were immersing themselves in a diverse array of classes in which they pursued artistic activities, such as singing the lieder of Franz Schubert, or studying the tea ceremony or flamenco dancing. While some pursued these activities in private one-on-one classes, more often than not these women, and also older men, practiced these activities in large groups where they learned and performed together. Many students were retirees or were expecting to enter retirement in the near future. My curiosity was piqued. What was this culture of learning about? Who were these students, many of them women, who poured their time, significant amounts of money, and physical and emotional energies into these classes?

This book is a study of women's cultivation of self in later life within communities of learning in urban Japan.

During the past three decades, the Japanese government has shown remarkable interest in supporting learning among older persons. The term lifelong learning (*shōgai gakushū*) entered Japanese policy discussions after a UNESCO conference on adult education in 1965. This conference spearheaded a growing interest within Japan in learning across the life-course. In the same year, the government introduced classes (*kōreisha kyōshitsu*) for citizens over the age of sixty (Koike 2003). In 1971, the government's Special Council on Social Education (*Shakai Kyōiku Shingikai*) published a report raising the many reasons why learning activities were necessary for older citizens. Among them were the maintenance of health, creation of social networks, and enrichment of leisure time (Koike 2003, 106). The Japanese government's expansion of programs for the aged in the 1970s was one of the largest and most rapid policy shifts that occurred in any industrialized nation in the postwar period (Campbell 1992). In 1984, the prime minister's office established a special council on lifelong learning, and in 1990, the Japanese Diet enacted the Law for the Promotion of Lifelong Learning (Shiraishi 1998; Ogawa 2009). The Japanese state today promotes lifelong learning as a means of ensuring an active senior population. It considers participation in group learning activities important in reducing the risk of ill-health associated with sedentary lifestyles, delaying the onset of senility, and indirectly reducing the burden on the national health insurance system. By framing the quest for lifelong learning in the language of individual initiative (*jihatsuteki ishi*), it also places emphasis on learning as a moral choice that individuals should make in order to remain healthy citizens of society.

Later Life Body-Based Learning Activities

Learning activities, often undertaken in circles (*saakuru*) or groups (*kai*), engage many Japanese citizens over age sixty. For example, in 2011, 17.4 percent of Japanese over sixty were engaged in learning activities (Cabinet Office, Government of Japan 2012, 42). Many public and private institutions in Japan offer learning opportunities specifically for older adults. This growth trend in opportunities for older persons to engage in learning activities is likely to expand in the future.

As John Traphagan (2000, 2006) states in his research on Japanese senior citizens who learn gateball (a sport that can be likened to croquet), many senior citizens have a strong wish to avoid dependency. For these senior citizens, the benefits of gateball are rarely phrased in terms of the importance of simply remaining physically fit in old age. Rather, the benefit and motive for undertaking these activities is articulated in explicitly moral and interpersonal terms, such as seniors wanting to remain participating members of the local community to avoid becoming a burden on their families. They engage in gateball in order to sustain a social self, which in turn, is considered important for well-being. Traphagan states that "life itself is a kind of normative task that requires . . . commitment and endurance" (2000, 158). One must persevere (*gambaru*) until the end. From the perspective of older persons, "failure to give one's all in the goal of preventing or at least delaying the onset of *boke* (senility) is a failure to carry out one's responsibility to develop capacities to the fullest" (ibid.). The consequence of becoming senile is to become a burden to family members and to society as a whole, so that use of social services becomes necessary. As Susan Long (2012, 132) also states, there is an increasingly normative value associated with being independent in old age in Japan. Older persons resist dependency. They are encouraged to remain self-reliant in old age by engaging in preventive health care, and embracing the use of technologies and assistive devices that will enable them to remain in their own homes rather than move into nursing care institutions.

This ethnography casts a spotlight on older women who learn Noh chanting and dance as an amateur (*shirôto*) activity. It focuses on the embodied training of a group of close to eighty amateur Noh dancers with whom I conducted fieldwork in 2004 and 2005, and in 2011 in Tokyo, Japan. It analyzes the way the body becomes the medium through which women articulate and craft their devotion to a *particular way of life*. They sculpt specific aspects of their physical being's capacities through activities such as chanting, the slow dance of Noh, and drumming. Typically, the chant and dance repertoire is excerpted from a Noh play and expresses a particular story line. The chant is a form of intoned storytelling. The pinnacle of this training is an hour-long performance at the Noh theater, where women perform wearing centuries-old costumes and masks.

Learning as a Space of Personal and Social Transformation

The amateur practice of Noh must be contextualized in other kinds of amateur (*shirôto*) activities. Barbara Rowland Mori, who has studied Japanese women's adoption of tea ceremony, states that practicing tea ceremony provides women with fulfillment (Mori 1991, 95). Tea ceremony is a socially sanctioned way for women to invest in their own education and engage in personal improvement (Mori 1991, 95–96). Often they take courses in related fields: calligraphy, poetry, history, and literature. Women learn how to choose, put on, and care for the kimono used during tea ceremony. Students and teachers make utensils and learn the variety and history of various crafts. Mori argues that this extensive education in various arts creates an image of the learner of the tea ceremony as "intelligent, cultured, talented, and worthy of esteem" (1991, 94). Furthermore, qualifying as tea ceremony practitioners provides women with a significant degree of autonomy and control over their lives. Women who become teachers set their own hours, choose their own students, and control their work environment to an extent that they might not otherwise enjoy, and many find this preferable to taking on a job in a firm or joining a family business. Through these activities, women can exert some influence on one of the major streams of art and esthetics in Japan, and gain the respect of the community for their involvement in this art form.

Etsuko Kato, also writing about Japanese women who practice tea ceremony, states that participation in this art form confers respect because learning tea ceremony involves embodying physical and mental disciplines, and discipline is highly valued in Japanese culture. In earlier historical periods the ceremony was associated with men of high status, such as the "Shogun, Emperor, aristocrats . . . wealthy merchants . . . [and] early modern industrialists," who partook of it as a leisure activity; this history confers additional prestige on women's pursuits (Kato 2004, 191). As guardians and re-presenters of this esteemed tradition, the women gain an elevated status in society. Kato observes that this cultural capital in turn enables women to "equilibrate" themselves with their male family members. By mastering the techniques of preparing and serving tea, women close the educational gap between themselves and the male members of their families.

In her study of vacations that focus on the craft of silk weaving, Millie Creighton approaches learning silk weaving as a form of personal expression and self-development. She explains that the act of participating in a traditional craft vacation is a source of pride for these women because it signals to others that they have discretionary use of their time and funds. Because of the value placed on learning in Japanese culture, the fact that it is taken up as an educational pursuit is accorded social respect. While doing silk weaving does not confer gender equality in terms of the income that the women earn from their jobs, women interpret such activities as enhancing their control over their time, activities, and avenues of personal expression (Creighton 2001, 26). These seminars reflect women's attempts to recapture traditionally female realms of activity. Women take pride in their involvement in an educational hobby historically associated with women's work.

Embedded in these studies of leisure is the notion that practitioners of leisure find it fulfilling because it confers social respectability and increases women's status. The classical theorist of leisure Thorstein Veblen and the sociologist Pierre Bourdieu explored leisure practices through this frame of distinction, claiming that esteemed leisure practices enable people who participate in them to layer a new identity onto their existing ones and, in doing so, to elevate their social status and establish social distinction (Bourdieu 1984, 57). Veblen (1991[c.1899]), in his classic work on leisure of the affluent class, *The Theory of the Leisure Class,* argued that individuals are motivated by the desire to acquire a status distinction. He approached the pursuit of leisure activities, such as collecting rare dogs and horses and appreciating music, as a means for establishing social distinction. Similarly, in his study of taste, *Distinction: A Social Critique of the Judgment of Taste,* Bourdieu observed that acts of consumption—such as the appreciation of household interiors, artwork, and cuisine—serve to establish and sustain social status. "Aesthetic stances adopted in matters like cosmetics, clothing, or home decoration are opportunities to experience or assert one's position in social space, as rank to be upheld or as distance to be kept" (1984, 55).

While I agree that these types of gains in distinction are important, my fieldwork demonstrates that an analysis of leisure activities that is oriented toward exploring the social distinction, cultural capital, and social respectability associated with participating in leisure practices provides only a partial view of the gains practitioners derive from these activities. The appeal of Noh comes as much from other processes, for example, the peeling away of identity and the emergence of new states of self. This is in contrast to an identity arising from the everyday self as a social institution that goes on accumulating more responsibility, knowledge, and respectability throughout life. These all become layers of everyday identity. The self that is attached to this identity becomes a personal as well as a public reality. Through leisure activities, however, practitioners can detach from this everyday identity. With the peeling away of identity that occurs, practitioners gain an opportunity to expand the concept of who they are and who they can become.

The ethnography thus delves into this process of the formation and dissolution of identity and the creation of new selves, using the case study of Noh. I argue that such formation and dissolution of selfhood are an important part of the journey in later life. I see these processes as what gives meaning to life. Whereas most scholars of women's leisure draw attention to identity formation, and specifically the gains in social respectability, associated with participating in leisure practices, I place emphasis on both the formation of identities, and on the dissolution of identities and emergence of new states of self that arise from self-awareness facilitated by immersion in leisure.

Robert Stebbins (2006, 113) uses the idea of "serious leisure" to describe leisure activities that require perseverance, significant personal effort, use of the body, and a quest for self-actualization. Stebbins's conception of leisure appropriately captures the seriousness attached to the practice of Noh that makes it a pathway of disciplined practice leading to self-actualization rather than simply a form of relaxation. These leisure activities are "enduring pursuits with their own background contingencies, histories of turning points, and stages of achievement or involvement" (Stebbins 2006, 6). They involve long-term engagement and commitment. Serious leisure enthusiasts often make a "career" of their endeavors; however, these careers are seldom paid professions. If anything, they often entail a considerable financial investment by the practitioner, with no expectation of financial return.

Betsy Wearing's analysis of leisure is also useful here. She argues that we can conceptualize leisure in terms of social spaces that allow for modes of being that are different from those of the everyday constraints of human life (1998, ix). Examining the writing activities of the Pacific Islander author Grace Mera Molisa, Wearing states that the act of writing poetry is a way for Molisa and women like her to express their thoughts and experiences (1998, 167). Writing poetry is both a space of resistance to male domination and a space for her own enlargement or growth. Wearing's use of the term *space* instead of the word *action* is strategic; it derives from the influence of the feminist geographer Doreen Massey, who suggests that we think of space in relational terms. Moreover, inherent in this notion of "space" is process, where something is generated relationally through acts such as writing, speaking, performing, and communicating. These women create spaces of pleasure by talking, sharing poetry, and humor. These spaces restore to women a sense of self-worth and community. In some cases, they take on political dimensions by serving as a venue for making marginalized people visible and their voices heard; in other cases they serve as a node for forging solidarity or coalition movements with others.

Inspired by this analysis, which examines leisure activity as a relational field of personal growth and social transformation, I examine the desires and motivations of the women who take up Noh. I do so to explore the argument that leisure pursuits are an important medium of self-actualization especially in later life.

Fieldwork

Soon after my arrival in Tokyo in the winter of 2004, I found an apartment in the city of Musashi Koganei in western Tokyo within thirty minutes' commute of the central hub of Shinjuku. Musashi Koganei is located on the Musashino Plain and has a number of universities, small businesses, parks, and homes. I lived within five minutes' walk of a Zen nunnery which served simple yet exquisite vegetarian temple food. The abbess of the nunnery, Yoshino Kōbun, and the head chef, Nishida Ayako, who was formerly a chef of French cuisine, welcomed me to the temple.[1] In the first few months of fieldwork, I went to the temple each week to meet with the two women to discuss the progress of my findings. The abbess and chef were friendly and eager to take on the role of sponsors in my study of women's later life learning. They sought in myriad ways to assist me by introducing me to friends they felt might advance my research. Their circles of associates were diverse and included teachers of various Japanese cultural arts such as flower arrangement and the tea ceremony. The temple was like a village green where there was a constant flow of people, primarily women, who gathered to seek counsel from the abbess for difficulties with their in-laws and husbands. Others came to the temple to chat with the jovial chef, Ayako, who had once run her own French cooking school and continued to welcome her former students to the nunnery.

In addition to the space of the nunnery, I sought to maximize my opportunities to meet a diverse array of women and men in their sixties. I identified school reunions as one of my primary channels of research. I drew on Theodore Bestor's (2003:315) advice to "choose a network, not a neighborhood." I went to high school and college reunions where I met women and men in their sixties. At each of these reunions, I introduced myself and my research on retirees and conversed with the participants. I followed up with select members who expressed interest in participating in the research. Many were involved in later life learning activities, such as learning to play the flute at a music school.

The Zen temple proved to be a place of serendipitous encounters. It was here that I met the teacher of the Sumire Kai (Violet Group), Tsurumi Reiko, at the birthday celebration of the abbess. At this event, Tsurumi sang and played her shoulder drum (*kotsuzumi*). She was a vibrant and dynamic seventy-eight-year-old woman who performed with three women students in their fifties and sixties. I approached Tsurumi to explain that I was researching later life learning activities. She seemed taken that a "foreigner" wanted to learn Noh and enthusiastically welcomed me to her class.

My analysis of the embodied training that the women undertake at the Sumire Kai training center is based on a large body of observational and experiential data produced in the course of my ethnographic study. I joined a class where all of the students were women, and hence much of the analysis in this ethnography centers on women and their embodied practice. At the center, I trained regularly with them, spending hours learning how to chant Noh plays, master dance steps, and play the shoulder drum. Together we prepared for recitals and staged performances at the Noh Theater.

In time, I conducted more than fifty in-depth life history interviews with the women, including the teacher, Tsurumi Sensei. We also had informal conversations at airports, trains, hotels, coffee shops, and everywhere that our Noh training took us. Some interactions occurred in the women's homes.

My participation in the training activities and recitals of the Sumire Kai was a crucial building block for creating relationships within which communication became possible. My experience with the Noh group confirms that repeated encounters in a variety of contexts generate the trust that is crucial to informants speaking with candor. Gaining that trust is not simply a means to the end of gaining good data, but is part of the ethics of anthropology: to respect the sacredness of another life and to respect its specificity. The anthropological research process, perhaps more than any other research endeavor, relies on the delicate exchange between the researcher and informant, and on the informant's willingness to entrust the researcher with the "intimacy of [her] life" (Kleinman 1988, 237).

Shoulder Drum

From early in my childhood, my maternal grandmother, Sotomi Sadako, was a force of discipline, arriving often at my home in Tokyo, where I grew up, to stay with my parents and my sister and me. I always felt she was scolding me for being slipshod in my ways. But as I grew older, our relationship changed: from being simply a forbidding presence, she also became an inspiration to me. In her seventies she opened a museum to showcase the work of artists who were involved in the Japanese traditional arts and crafts, especially material arts such as ceramics and textiles. Her commitment to sustaining these arts through sponsorship of contemporary artists was evident in her tireless dedication to creating opportunities for these artists to exhibit their work.

She herself was a skilled calligrapher and a creative craftswoman, making packets of writing paper out of *fusuma* (sliding door) paper samples with grace, speed, and precision: each packet contained sheets of writing paper that she had carefully stamped and packaged into handmade envelopes, and tied with gold and silver bows. When I told my grandmother on a visit to her home in Kobe that I had begun to learn Noh chanting as part of my fieldwork, and was studying women who were amateur practitioners of Noh, her response took me by surprise. She stated, quite adamantly, that Noh chanting was so arcane and esoteric that unless I really enjoyed doing it, I should not pursue it. She continued in this vein. "Even a Japanese person cannot appreciate Noh." (*Nihonjin de sae Noh ga wakaranai no ni naze anta ga benkyô suru no.*) The words implied a primacy of understanding given to Japanese; if even Japanese "natives" could not understand or appreciate Noh's depths, then how could I, who was half Japanese, even possibly try?

On my return from her home in Kobe, I was surprised to find a package awaiting me. Inside the box was, of all things, a letter and shoulder drum that my grandmother said I could use in my Noh class. My grandmother wrote, "This is a shoulder drum that my father gave my sister and me when we were teenagers in the girls' school in 1920. It is yours to keep. It takes three years for even one segment of a bamboo to grow. Give Noh at least three years and see what happens." This book explains the journey that my encounter with the amateur world of Noh has taken.

Outline of Chapters

The learning community of the Sumire Kai is both an object of study and a window through which I trace the negotiations of relationships and the production of selves. I invite the reader into some of the classrooms where I came to know these women both as a fellow student and as an ethnographer. These spaces offer various insights into the social construction of gender roles in retirement and their impact on women's identities. I also examine, through the various chapters, why and how embodied learning activities are empowering.

In chapter 1, "Amateur Noh Practitioners," I provide background on women in Noh and the practice of amateur learning of Noh. I situate the Sumire Kai learning community within the broader social and historical landscape of Noh. I take a novel approach to studying the institution of Noh by focusing on the invisible masses, the amateur female practitioners, who play a crucial role in sustaining this art in the twenty-first century.

In chapter 2, "The Biography of a Noh Teacher," I examine how the leader of the Noh group became a teacher of Noh chanting and dance. She pursued Noh leisure as one way to construct an identity independent of her housewife role. In later life, this lifelong immersion in Noh translates into a leadership position. I contextualize her life history within the lives of other middle-class women who enjoyed social and economic privilege in postwar Japan but found their lives restricted by their position as professional housewives. I illuminate her involvement in the arts as a path to empowerment.

In chapter 3, "Rituals of Learning," I delve into the pedagogy of the Sumire Kai, examining the women who train there. I provide an analysis of how this leisure activity serves as a pathway for self-actualization. I describe the rituals of learning within which women pursue self-actualization and examine their commentaries on why self-actualization is important to them in later life.

In chapter 4, "Peeling Away of Identity," I offer further insights into the lifeworld of the amateur Noh practitioner. I argue that to understand what compels these women to devote hundreds of hours toward training to dance and sing, one must explore the corporeal effects of these activities and analyze the experiential states that are facilitated through repetitive practice and cultivation of the body. These experiential states, in turn, have important benefits on the everyday lives and identities of these amateur women practitioners. The chapter also examines the Sumire Kai's search for a successor to Tsurumi Sensei and finally returns to Tsurumi Sensei's assertion that she will never stop learning.

In chapter 5, "Acceptance," I engage in a reflection on the process of letting go of attachment to egoic self. I explore the theme of acceptance, drawing on a vignette of a woman, Yoshiko, who is training to be a nun in western Japan. I argue that an integral aspect of the expansion of self discussed in the previous chapter is the acceptance of the otherness of the self.

In the Conclusion, I recapitulate the central argument of the ethnography, about the role that learning can play in facilitating this process of growth in later life. I examine questions of identity and its fluidity, as well as upheaval and transition and, following this transition, the creation of new identities. The conclusion considers what other societies may learn from these Japanese women who adopt embodied practice in dance and chanting as a mode of lifelong learning and as a way to forge a meaningful old age.

Note

1. As I describe in more detail later, these names are pseudonyms, as are most names in this book. With the exception of government officials and other public figures whose names and behavior are a matter of public record, the names of all of the people I researched have been changed. This is meant to ensure confidentiality and protect the anonymity of individuals, families, and institutions involved. All translations from Japanese to English are mine unless otherwise indicated.

1

Amateur Noh Practitioners

Noh is a form of classical Japanese theater that dates back to the fourteenth century. Combining elements of dance, drama, music, and poetry, it is characterized by a rich interplay of symbolism, music and dance, and masks and costumes (Yasuda 1984, 1). Noh's subject matter is taken mainly from Japan's classical literature, such as the *Manyôshu, The Tale of the Heike,* and *The Tale of Genji.*[1] Noh is an important feature of Japanese heritage and has been accorded state protection. The Japanese government designates especially accomplished Noh actors as Important Intangible Cultural Properties. This designation was made official through the 1950 Protection of Cultural Assets Law (*bunkazai hogo-hō*), which added the category Intangible Cultural Properties, popularly known as "Living National Treasures" (*ningen kokuhō*), to the list of protected works of art and architecture. Under the Law for the Protection of Cultural Properties, Intangible Cultural Properties are defined as "drama, music, craft techniques and other cultural products, which possess a high historical or artistic value for Japan. . . . [T]he fundamental difference between intangible and tangible Cultural Properties is that Intangible Cultural Properties are not the products of the techniques practiced by individuals or groups, but are skills, behaviors, and actions of people" (Agency for Cultural Affairs of Japan 2008b, 9). This designation affords a degree of state protection to a national tradition as well as to some of its actors. In 2001, UNESCO proclaimed Noh to be an Intangible Cultural Heritage of Humanity, and the Japan

Arts Council nurtures successors of this theatrical style. In spite of this level of support, Noh is experiencing a steady decline in the number of enthusiasts, especially among the younger generations of Japanese (Horikami 2010, 19).

There has been extensive academic interest in Noh plays, performance practices, and history (Keene and Tyler 1970; Klein 1991: Terasaki 2002; Brown 2001; Wakita 2005). Still under-studied, however, is the involvement of amateur practitioners, especially women, in this art form. The amateur practitioner is a very important element of Noh that is often crowded out by the narratives of famous performers' lives and discussions of Noh's place in Japanese culture (Okamoto 2008, 136; Geilhorn 2008; Uzawa 2008). Both professionals and the institution of Noh as a whole depend on amateur practitioners to sustain them, but this fact is rarely acknowledged. This book provides an analysis of the role of amateur engagement in Noh drama and the efforts of amateurs to practice Noh as a vehicle for personal development. Before discussing the amateur woman practitioner, I provide a brief history of the involvement of women in Noh drama.

Brief History of Women in Noh

Japanese women were involved in Noh from very early in its history. Accounts of women appearing in Noh can be found, for example, in the diary of Prince Fushimi no Miya Sada-fumi, which dates back to 1432. The entry describes a series of benefit performances (*kanjin noh*) in which women performed (Teele 2002, 68). Women's public performance of Noh ended in the 1600s when the Tokugawa shogunate placed general restrictions on women's participation in the performing arts. In 1629, it prohibited all public performances by women in Noh, and meanwhile continued to support and encourage men's Noh troupes. Noh became almost exclusively a male theatrical art and recreational activity that was restricted primarily to high-status men. Successive feudal regimes and government leaders from the fourteenth to the twentieth centuries used Noh to bolster their authority and dominion (Rath 2004; Brown 2001). Noh became a crucible of political power centering on status and cultural capital. Japanese political leaders formed alliances with the hereditary leaders of the Noh schools (*iemoto*) and turned Noh into an elite male esthetic that set it apart from other social groups and other forms of cultural performance, including the Kabuki theater.

Women were prohibited from entering the ranks of professionals until the twentieth century. The first modern woman to become a professional Noh actor was Tsumura Kimiko, who performed in the Noh Theater in the 1930s and 1940s (Kanamori 1994, 140). Her Noh debut, in 1939, was in a performance of *Ataka,* a play based on the epic struggle of the warring Genji and Heike clans in the twelfth century. This was an important event in the history of women's entry into professional Noh. In 1948, Tsumura became one of five women to enter the *Nohgaku* Performers' Association (*Nohgaku Kyōkai*), and was recognized as a professional performer by the Kanze school of Noh.

Meanwhile, by the 1920s, wives and daughters of elite men came to practice Noh as "one of the proper accomplishments" appropriate for cultured young women (Teele 2002, 69). The scholar Ikenouchi Nobuyoshi, writing in the journal *Nôgaku,* advocated Noh for the physical and cultural education of young women (Ikenouchi in Rath 2004, 106). Noh dance, chanting, and playing of musical instruments became part of the list of accomplishments, including the tea ceremony and flower arrangement, that young women studied before marriage.

Today, women actors are still a small minority, although they make up a larger proportion of the professional world of Noh than ever before. In 2013, women made up approximately 15 percent of the *Nohgaku* Performers' Association, which had 1,262 members (*Nohgaku* Performers' Association 2013). Among these women are professional actors, semiprofessional performers, and those certified as licensed instructors (*shihan*) by their schools. This ethnography examines the life and *kai* of a female performer certified by the Hosho School, one of the five schools of Noh.

In the late 1940s and early 1950s, Noh schools began to welcome significant numbers of amateur women practitioners.[2] This increase in their numbers was related to the upheaval of World War II and the broader societal changes that followed. The democratization movements of that era, which led to the dismantling of major business conglomerates (*zaibatsu*) and stripping of wealth and titles from the Japanese nobility known as the *kazoku,* dealt a blow to the Noh world (Lebra 1993). Noh actors and teachers lost some of their former patrons, and some feared that if the Noh schools did not target new social groups they would decline into oblivion (Ejima 1967, 2).

In response, the *iemoto* of, for example, the Hosho School, Hosho Kuro, launched an active campaign in the late 1940s and early 1950s to build a new clientele of Noh amateurs. He set out to increase the total number of Hosho Noh enthusiasts to one million people. A major concept that informed this quest for new practitioners was widening the base (*susono o hirogeru*) of the pyramid. In the postwar years, the Noh schools packaged their received knowledge and marketed their traditions to amateur students, including housewives, university students, and salaried employees of companies (Moore 2012). These students were not wealthy patrons but were part of the rapidly expanding middle class. The Hosho *iemoto* also established the Association of *Shokutaku* (*Shokutaku Kai*) to increase the number of licensed first-level teachers of Noh. These licenses certify them to teach their own students, thereby helping to expand the Hosho School.

By the 1970s, Noh chanting (*utai*), in particular, had become a thriving recreational activity in Japan (Bethe and Brazell 1982). Tens of thousands of amateurs studied chanting, and amateur recitals were held regularly. Radio stations broadcast weekly programs of Noh chanting. At weddings and social occasions, people often chanted selections from Noh plays. The number of amateur enthusiasts reached a peak in the 1980s, after which it has slowly declined. Noh has since been losing enthusiasts, particularly among the younger generations of Japanese.

In the past, the value of Noh theater was invoked in terms of its elite associations, gentility, and patronage by highly placed officials and patrons, such as Iwakura Tomomi in the early Meiji period (Nishiyama 1982, 364). While these inflections of class and gentility remain, they are not the only qualities that define Noh for these contemporary practitioners. Rather, these practitioners point to the qualities of slow and sustained learning, abiding with patience, and—for the older women featured in this book— Noh's contribution to personal development. In this book we take a look into their world and see what they gain from Noh.

Amateur Women Practitioners

In the world of Noh, the distinction between professionals and amateurs is very clearly defined. Professional actors (*kurōto*) have attained high levels of certification and stage plays at the various theaters around Japan. The *shirôto*, or amateurs, practice Noh as a leisure activity. Their training in Noh dance (*shimai*), singing (*utai*), and instruments *(hayashi)* is generally not a stepping stone to a professional acting career on the Noh stage. Yet, like many other hobbyists in traditional arts such as tea ceremony or calligraphy, Noh amateurs take their practice seriously and devote many years to it.

Women make up the majority of amateur Noh practitioners (Teele 2002, 70). A few go on to gain licenses such as the *shokutaku* and the *jun shokubun* license, both of which certify them to teach their own students.[2] Robert Stebbins's conception of serious leisure appropriately captures the seriousness attached to the practice of Noh that makes it a pathway of dedicated effort rather than simply a form of relaxation.

Amateurs occupy a distinct and important place in the world of Noh practitioners in contemporary Japan. Their patronage of Noh takes the form of both spectatorship, which is a subsidiary part of their training, and studentship, learning Noh from more highly trained practitioners. They attend classes, purchase costumes and instruments for training, perform in recitals, and pay fees to the Noh theater and to the professional actors who participate in their recitals. Many want Noh to thrive, even though as amateurs they do not have official responsibility to ensure that Noh continues into the future. To that end, they are involved in public campaigns that lobby the Japanese government to increase its spending on the cultural arts.

Keikogoto

The primary aspect of amateur Noh practice that I explore in this ethnography is called *keikogoto*. It refers to the learning a student undertakes with the guidance of a teacher, and also the practice the individual undertakes in between sessions with the teacher. It is generally funded privately by the individual and requires a certain level of financial flexibility on the part of the learner. Terms that have approximately the same meaning as *keikogoto* are *naraigoto* (things that are learned) and *ressun* (lessons). *Keikogoto* and *naraigoto* usually refer to activities of Japanese derivation such as Japanese dance (*Nihon buyô*), calligraphy (*shûji*), Noh singing (*utai*), and flower arrangement (*ikebana*). The term *ressun* usually refers to activities of a non-Japanese derivation such as classical ballet, piano, or violin.

When asked what gives meaning to Noh, many amateurs say that it is the actual training that matters most, that it is their involvement in the rigors of Noh practice that keeps them returning to Noh. What does this world feel like? My aim is to offer insight into the lifeworld of one group of amateur Noh practitioners, to explore what compels women to devote hundreds of hours to this practice. I use a phenomenological approach to interpret these women's "being-in-the-world" through their descriptions of their sensory experiences (Fraleigh 2000, 59). The bodily experience of these feeling states engenders a commitment to Noh in these amateur enthusiasts.

The shift in focus from respectability to embodied experience, facilitated through Noh dance and chanting, has implications for how we understand the value of tradition in everyday life. Practitioners gain meaning by participating in and experiencing the ongoing life of tradition through embodying it, and experiencing its effects on their lives, rather than simply valuing it as a marker of their social identity. When they are embodying tradition, they are in what Mircea Eliade (1971 [1954], 149) calls "eternal" time: the distinction between past and present is suspended, and practitioners are in contact with being.

The Sumire Kai Noh Group

Tsurumi Reiko, who gained her first Noh qualification, the *shokutaku* license, in her thirties and her second qualification, the *jun shokubun* license, in her late fifties, established the Sumire Kai in 1986. She is trained in the Kôryu School of *kotsuzumi*. As the founder and teacher of the Sumire Kai, Tsurumi Sensei is responsible for transmitting the art of Noh to her students. Tsurumi Sensei has eighty students under her wing, and she travels frequently by plane and train to central and southern Japan to teach. She stages large Noh recitals for her students each spring and autumn. She is a busy and active member of the wider Noh world and maneuvers her way confidently within a social network of Noh actors, theater directors, and publishers. Tsurumi Sensei's students are important patrons who sustain the tradition of Noh through their own training.

Seventy percent of the Sumire Kai's eighty members are women, and their average age is sixty. Its student composition represents the contemporary demographic of Noh enthusiasts in Japan: predominantly female and over age fifty. The Sumire Kai's primary classroom is located in Tokyo near Shinjuku. The Sumire Kai has satellite classes in the cities of Kofu, Fuji-Yoshida, Fukuoka, Kumamoto, Kagoshima, and Miyazaki in eastern and southern Japan.

What gives direction to women's training is the schedule of recitals that is organized around the seasons of spring and autumn. This cyclicality of performances, and the extensive repertoire of plays that students seek to master, creates a sense that students are moving upward in an ever-stretching spiral of learning. Every second spring, the Sumire Kai hosts a large two-day recital at the Hosho School's official Noh stage in Suidobashi in Tokyo. Students perform to the accompaniment of professional Noh actors, some of whom are Intangible Cultural Properties, and the *iemoto*. A number of the students who have accumulated long years of practice and whom the teacher deems ready to stage a full-scale Noh play do so. In this hour-long performance they are dressed in full Noh costume and a mask.

This Noh performance at the Noh Theatre is the culmination of years of rigorous training in dancing and chanting. In the days leading up to these recitals, there is a huge crescendo of activity as students practice their performance, select their costumes, and send out invitations to friends and family. This high intensity

Figure 1.1. Performance of *Tōboku.* Courtesy of Kobayashi Kan.

of practice then subsides after each recital. During the first class following a recital, students share photos, reminisce about the recital and the most memorable performances, and select their next play.

Women in the Sumire Kai describe the significance of taking up a learning activity in a variety of ways. Some say they undertake *keiko* out of the desire to acquire a specific skill. Others speak of the desire to incorporate a particular discipline into the body through physical and vocal training. In the Japanese traditional performing arts, one is considered to acquire a particular skill and transform the body through this acquisition at the same time. Some women say they value the camaraderie and the social rewards that come from being part of a group pursuing a shared activity. Others state that engaging in these activities allows them to strive for something that was not associated with their role in the workplace or the family. It is an opportunity to create a life independent of their lives as workers or as women tied to the home. For those women who are grandmothers, they are also eager to have an active life distinct from their familial roles.

The practice of Noh actors teaching amateurs was established in the eighteenth century. It was established across a wide range of traditional arts beyond Noh and is tied to the establishment of the *iemoto* system. As Eric Rath explains in his extensive analysis of the establishment of Noh as a social institution, Noh's traditions were contested at various times over many centuries. These contests led to Noh being transformed from a medieval entertainment practiced by both women and men into a "classic art performed by a closed profession dominated by a select elite" (2004, 6–8). The eighteenth-century establishment of the *iemoto* system was a pivotal moment in this process. The family head came to be esteemed as the supreme practitioner and teacher of his art. Nishiyama Matsunosuke (1982) explains that the family head system marketed Noh as a hobby, a possible vocation, and a form of spiritual cultivation.

To this day, the family head system links heredity with expertise and asserts dominion by claiming exclusive access to profound knowledge because of direct descent from the school's patriarch. Authority depends on bloodlines. The licenses conferred on teachers are approved by the family head and can be understood as certificates given to advanced students to acknowledge their attaining skill in chanting, dancing, or playing instruments. Different licenses are issued for different levels of training in recognition of students' mastery of skills appropriate to that level. Licensing gives schools a means to regulate the transmission of key skills. The licenses have a gatekeeping function: they keep those who are less skilled from rising in the hierarchy. By controlling amateur access to licenses, schools seek to preserve the school's highest knowledge and skills (Rath 2004, 194). They earn revenues from licensing fees. Such instruments for regulating amateur involvement also help the family head to control the activities of lower-ranking professionals in the school by clarifying the hierarchies of power and knowledge. This influences how Noh teachers such as Tsurumi maintain good ties with their colleagues. This is a topic I develop in the next chapter, where I examine the life history of the Noh teacher of the Sumire Kai.

Conclusion

This chapter has provided an overview of the social world of Noh and the distinction between Noh actors and amateurs. It has provided a history of the increased presence of women in this theater as both actors and amateurs. After being excluded from professional performances for hundreds of years, increasing numbers of women became Noh professionals in the course of the twentieth and twenty-first centuries. These professionals have cultivated their own female students. The Sumire Kai Noh teacher and her group can be situated within the broader social history of Noh. I take my own approach to studying the institution of Noh by focusing on women performers and the invisible masses, the amateur female practitioners, who play a crucial role in sustaining this art in the twenty-first century. The next chapter explores the teacher's biography and the way she practices Noh as a vehicle for self-actualization.

Notes

1. The *Manyôshu* ("Collection of Ten Thousand Leaves") is the oldest existing collection of Japanese poetry, compiled sometime between the eighth and twelfth centuries. The *The Tale of the Heike* is an epic account of the struggle between the Minamoto (Genji) and Taira (Heike) clans to control Japan during the twelfth-century conflict known as the *Genpei War.* They were compiled from a collection of oral stories and transcribed in 1371, and are considered among the great

classics of medieval Japanese literature. These tales focus on the tragic experiences of characters caught in the conflict between the two great clans of medieval Japan. *The Tale of Genji*, a classic work of Japanese literature attributed to the Japanese noblewoman Murasaki Shikibu in the early eleventh century, features the story of Prince Genji and his relationships with women in the Japanese court.

2. Professional female Noh performers face significant barriers. They tend to have fewer opportunities to perform on the Noh stage and to build credit to be inducted into the *Nihon Nohgakukai,* the organization for Noh actors who are named Intangible Cultural Properties. Because one of the criteria for entry into the *Nihon Nohgakukai* is the staging of two or more performances of the main character (*shite*) role each year, the number of women actors who meet the criteria for entry into the Nohgakukai is significantly lower than male actors (Miyanishi 2005). For more discussion of the challenges women actors face, see Geilhorn 2008 and Uzawa 2008.

3. Different licenses are issued for different levels of training in recognition of students' mastery of skills appropriate to that level: for the Hosho school, the licenses are for the levels of *shokutaku, jun shokubun,* and *shokubun.* The Kanze school does not have the *shokutaku* license. The demarcation between professional and amateur in the Kanze school is maintained more strictly.

2

The Biography of a Noh Teacher

Tsurumi Reiko, the founder and *sensei* (teacher) of the Sumire Kai Noh group was seventy-eight years old at the time I met her. Our first encounter took place one spring day at a Zen nunnery in the suburb of Musashi Koganei in western Tokyo. Sensei and three of her women students had been invited to the nunnery as special guests to celebrate the abbess's birthday. She was five feet tall, rotund but small-boned, and had silver-grey hair tied in a bun on her head. With her posture upright and gaze focused, Sensei played the shoulder drum (*kotsuzumi*) and accompanied the women as they performed three short dances. To my untrained eye, the dance movements were slow and trancelike, and I began to feel somewhat sleepy. I might have dozed off had it not been for the pins and needles that shot through my feet after two hours of sitting with folded legs on the *tatami* floor. Once the performance ended, Sensei suddenly came forward. Although she had seemed at first glance like a cute grandmotherly figure, the kind of grandmother one might encounter in a Japanese fable or a Miyazaki Hayao animation film, she turned into a commanding presence.

"I shall now give you a lesson on how to chant *Crane and Tortoise*," she declared. A murmur rose in the room as I and the assembled guests, many of whom had never chanted a Noh play, considered this proposition. Before we could respond, she ordered us to arrange ourselves into three rows and directed one of her students to distribute sheets of Noh libretti. The libretti had no musical notation, at least not any that my training in classical piano had prepared me to read. All I could see were what appeared to resemble columns of ancient Japanese script flowing down the page like gentle waterfalls.

With Sensei's deep and powerful voice leading the way, the assembled guests began tuning up their voices. "*Ahhhh~~~~~~~~ Ahhhhh~~~~~~~~~~~.*" Sensei sat up at the front glaring sternly at the guests. I felt fortunate to be sitting in the back row because, at first, I could not stop chuckling. Next to me was a French woman who had been working as a kitchen hand in the temple. She could not stop giggling either. I tried my best to regain seriousness and stop chuckling as Sensei began to talk. She gave us some background on *Crane and Tortoise,* one of the first songs students learn in the Noh repertoire. It is often performed on felicitous occasions such as birthdays and weddings. In the song, the Tang emperor visits his Moon Pavilion to watch two courtiers dance as the spirits of the crane and tortoise. The crane is said to live for a thousand years, and the tortoise for ten thousand; they are traditional symbols of longevity.[1]

Sensei instructed some of us to take the role of the emperor and others the role of the courtier and still others the chorus. With Sensei's voice leading the way, we launched into the *Crane and Tortoise* song:

> How numerous the examples of things that last a
>   thousand ages.
> How numerous the examples of things that last a
>   thousand ages.
> What should we begin with?
> First, the tortoise, green as the small Princess Pine.
> When it dances, so does the red-crested crane.
> They give one thousand years of long life to our
>   lord.
> As they attend to the sovereign in the garden, the
>   lord's face spills over with joy.
> Their dance is truly delightful . . . .

Midway through the song, she boomed, "Breathe from your stomach and sing *LOUDER*."

Some of the assembled guests who had been singing tentatively were clearly overwhelmed by her zeal. By the time we reached the end of the play, I could feel a sense of relief pervade the room, only to be cut off as Sensei insisted, "One more time." We launched into the chanting again, this time knowing that we had to infuse the words of the emperor and courtier with more gusto.

Interestingly, I became increasingly immersed in the chanting and found myself enjoying it. When we neared the end of the song for the third time, Sensei declared, "*ONE MORE TIME*." And so we proceeded in this fashion, for two more rounds of *Crane and Tortoise*.

Once the surprise lesson had ended, we staggered off to the main temple to eat the celebratory meal, a special vegetarian meal served in small lacquerware boxes. The surprise lesson had left us feeling ravenous. Inside the boxes was an assortment of delicious Zen food: creamy "sesame tofu" made of ground sesame seeds, deep-fried eggplant halves spread with citron-flavored white miso, and tiny mountain yams wrapped in crisp seaweed. The other guests and I devoured the lunch.

While I felt relieved when the lesson ended, I could not shake the feeling of curiosity that bubbled up inside of me. I felt intrigued by Sensei's commitment to impart her own training to strangers. I sensed an immediacy and urgency in her teaching, almost a fury, that made her seem to leap out of her skin. The seriousness with which she sought to impart her craft to the guests captured my interest. She had unrelentingly taught the *Crane and Tortoise* again and again and again. Unperturbed by the giggles and the discomfort of her guests, she continued forth. Through the sheer force of her teaching, the space of the temple had been turned into a Noh classroom. There was a fearlessness about her that drew me in.

At the end of the birthday party, I decided to approach Tsurumi Sensei and explain to her that I was a doctoral student from an American university researching the lifestyles of Japanese men and women as they enter retirement. I asked rather boldly whether she had retirees in her class whom I could meet. Sensei immediately replied that she would welcome my visit and proceeded to write down all of her contact details.

This chapter explores Sensei's life and career as a Noh teacher. I relay stories Tsurumi Sensei shared with me. The stories provide insight into the moral debates about appropriate feminine roles of her time.

To understand the significance of Sensei developing a career as a Noh teacher, it is important to understand the Japanese family system of the postwar decades. It was a time when the life of the professional housewife (*sengyô shufu*), who dedicates herself to managing the home, gained ascendancy as an idealized way of life. Women like her were discouraged from taking up activities that put them in the paid labor force. Many had limited opportunities for public recognition of their personal efforts, and operated with gender norms that encouraged them to aid family members in gaining public recognition rather than seek that recognition themselves (see also Kato 2004). Tsurumi Sensei embraced this role of the professional housewife but also found it confining. By turning to Noh training, she was able to construct an identity independent of her housewife role and become a Noh teacher in late life.

She is a social actor who strategically uses the symbols and social constraints in her life to create a path of mobility over her life course. Like Robert Desjarlais (1996, 882), I posit that agency is not "original" or "foundational" to the individual; there is no agency without a set of practicalities and forums giving rise to the capacity for action.

The first half of this chapter traces Tsurumi Sensei's life. I provide an account of her childhood, the critical teenage years of initiation into Noh during World War II, her marriage and subsequent training in Noh. Her maternal uncle, who taught her to chant Noh plays in the paddy fields of southern Japan during that war, was a force that ignited her commitment to Noh training and to the transmission of this art form today. The latter half of this chapter analyzes strategic constructions of feminine selfhood. I focus in particular on the hyperbolic performance of womanhood through food. Tsurumi Reiko's capacity to succeed as a Noh pedagogue lies in more than her prodigious skill in performing and teaching chanting and dance. It also relies on the creation of gendered effects offstage, specifically her construction of an identity of a competent housewife. Here I argue that gender attributes are not expressive of a preexisting identity but performative. Gender reality is created through sustained social performances (Butler 1990).

Visiting the Sumire Kai

Two weeks after our first meeting, I visited Tsurumi Sensei's home. Clutching the small sheet of directions that she had given me, I made my way up the steps of the subway station and stepped out onto a busy main road. Buses, taxis, and cars sped by. I walked down the sidewalk, dodging bicycles. The directions said to walk past a convenience store and an Indonesian spices store, and to turn off this busy road into a small side street. Entering the small street, I walked a few steps until I came up to a white eight-story apartment building. The street number matched the address on my sheet, but had I come to the right place? Her home supposedly had a Noh stage in it but from the exterior of the building it was difficult to imagine anything like that inside.

Entering through the glass doors, I made my way into the foyer and up the linoleum-covered steps of the apartment building to the first landing. From one of the doors wafted the inviting aroma of fried sweet potatoes. I made my way up the next set of stairs to the third floor landing and walked around each of the doors until I found a tiny nameplate reading "Tsurumi."

Gingerly pulling open the door of the apartment, I found a jumble of maybe ten pairs of women's shoes in the small entryway. Removing mine, I stepped inside and opened a sliding door consisting of translucent white paper *(washi)* over a wooden frame. In the room was indeed a magnificent Noh practice stage, with gleaming wooden floors. At the rear of the stage was a representation of a large green pine tree, the centerpiece of the Noh stage. The room held an air of deep concentration. The calm interior space of this training center stood in sharp contrast to the hustle and bustle of the street below.

"Moore-san, you are finally here!" called out Tsurumi Sensei. Smartly dressed in a black and white zebra-striped shirt and black cotton slacks, she sprang up from her chair in the corner of the training center and walked toward me, carrying herself with poise and certainty. The women students who were seated in the training center bowed, as if to provide a gesture of acknowledgment, and then continued fine-tuning their drumming sequences or talking quietly among themselves.

Telling the women that she would take me to the common room on the second floor, Tsurumi Sensei led me out of the Noh practice room. We made our way down the staircase to the landing below and walked toward the door from which emanated the aroma of the sweet potatoes. Walking into the apartment, she led me into a large carpeted common room that had been comfortably set up as a place for students to dine together. "Sit down, sit down. Make yourself at home," she said. I seated myself at one of the low dining tables and gazed at a glass cabinet filled with large plates, teacups and saucers, and various bowls. It looked like enough chinaware to feed a crowd of fifty. Tsurumi Sensei went into the kitchen and soon reappeared carrying a tray with small bowls of steaming white rice and some blanched green beans, drizzled with a delicious-looking miso sauce. Kneeling onto the floor, she set the tray on the table and offered me the food. As I began to eat, Tsurumi Sensei, who enjoyed telling stories about herself, began to tell me about her life. She invited me to learn Noh chanting with her.

The following account of Sensei's life is based on a series of interviews and conversations I conducted with her over several months. A number of these conversations took place in the presence of other students of the Sumire Kai. Because I refer to Sensei in the days before she became a Noh teacher, I use her first name, Reiko.

Singing Near the Rice Paddy

Reiko's father died when she was five years old. Her father, who had been in poor health, succumbed to a tuberculosis epidemic that was raging through Japan in the 1930s. One month before Reiko's father died, the family doctor called her mother into the hospital room to deliver this warning: "Your husband does not have long to live. He is like an egg cracked open on a rock in the sea. One huge wave will wash over the rock, and the egg will go. You will need to care for your children by yourself."

Reiko's mother did not tell her children that their father was so sick. Instead, she told them that their father's work kept him busy and that he had to live somewhere else. Only in her late twenties, the mother prepared for the day when she would be the sole breadwinner for her small family, and enrolled in a midwifery school where she earned a license to deliver babies.

For the next decade, she raised her two children by herself in Miyazaki; then her husband's brother, Reiko's uncle, who had been living in Tokyo, returned with his wife. Reiko's uncle had held an illustrious position as a high court judge in Tokyo. But as Japan plunged more heavily into war in 1944, and as constant air raids threatened residents of Tokyo, he and his wife evacuated the city, leaving behind their home and virtually all of their possessions except some clothes and his Noh songbooks.

Meanwhile, at age sixteen, Reiko and her classmates were pulled out of school and worked each day in an ammunition factory, building weapons for the war. While the girls were working, the sirens would ring suddenly, signaling that the air raids had begun. The girls plunged into the nearby fields of wildflowers as the B-25s went roaring overhead. The bombers were apparently not meant to be targeting civilians, but because of the large munitions factory in Miyazaki city, they swooped through her village.

Each day after she finished working at the factory, Reiko and her uncle went to a field near the rice paddies and spread out a straw mat on the ground. He brought an armload of his songbooks, and they sat facing each other on this mat. They started with the most basic of plays, such as *Tsurukame* (Crane and Tortoise) and *Momijigari* (Maple Leaf Picking). Her uncle drilled her again and again on the basics of the rhythm of Noh. He was very severe in his demeanor, but he must have known his young niece found the sessions a chore and wanted instead to be playing with her friends at the beach.

One day, when Reiko's enthusiasm flagged, her uncle stopped teaching and shut the Noh songbooks. The two of them sat on the straw mats facing each other, as the sun beat down on them. "Reiko, people say that Japan will probably not win this war. And I think they are right. Our country is in deeply troubled times. People's sons, fathers, brothers are dying; many have left their homes like me. People everywhere are pawning their jewels and kimonos and anything of value in their homes— just so that they can buy some food to put on the table."

He continued, speaking of the possibility that Japan would lose its sovereignty: "One day soon you too might be forced to leave your home and to shed all of your possessions. And what will remain then? Possibly nothing. This is sad and frightening, perhaps, but there is something you need to understand. Possessions are ephemeral, they are superficial. Real cultivation is not about what you acquire and attach to yourself, as an adornment. It is the discipline that you imbue into your body. It is what will make you shine. No matter what strife befalls you, polish your voice and dancing. Chant, Reiko! Chant. This art will create a luster from within that nothing and nobody can take away from you. Your art (*gei*) will shine from within you."

Roland Barthes (1984), speaking of the experience of looking at photographs, differentiates between the *studium* and the *punctum*. The punctum is the element that "rises from the scene, shoots out of it like an arrow, and pierces me" (1984, 26). It is that "accident which pricks me (but also bruises me, is poignant to me)." For me, the prick comes in the form of a story, rather than a photograph. It is the story of Reiko's uncle that strikes me with its vividness. In this story, I can most clearly feel her stake in teaching Noh. When I heard Tsurumi Sensei tell this story, I was struck by the poignancy of the tale. Here was a man in midlife who had lost his job and been evacuated from his home to return to his natal village. He felt an impending sense of crisis as darkness loomed over the country. All around him the world was changing and people were losing everything they had attained. What was he to hang on to? What would be his compass?

For Reiko's uncle, it was the practice of Noh chanting and dance that was paramount. He wanted to pass on the one thing that he knew no one would take away. What he shared was what had been important for him personally in riding the waves and vicissitudes of life. Noh chanting was a source of joy for him, and it was meaningful to remain involved in Noh chanting and dancing when material circumstances were changing rapidly. He lost other things and discovered they were ephemeral; meanwhile, Japan was going through a lot of social upheaval and there was a leveling of material differences and circumstances.

The war ended, and at age eighteen Reiko graduated from girls' school (*jogakkō*). Her mother enrolled her in various classes such as cooking and sewing, to groom her for marriage. She also continued to learn Noh chanting and dance. Reiko's mother had found life as a single working woman extremely tough and did not want her daughter to endure what she had. She wanted her to marry and have what she believed would be a comfortable and sheltered life. Reiko took the lessons and also found a job as an assistant instructor in the home economics department of her school in Miyazaki. Through her culinary lessons, she discovered she had a knack for cooking. She taught girls how to make traditional Japanese dishes and newly popular Western dishes, which had been banned during the war.

Early Married Life

When Reiko was twenty-two, her uncle, who had become like a surrogate father, arranged for her to marry a young man called Tsurumi Jiro. Mr. Tsurumi was the second son of a family from Kagoshima, the prefecture neighboring Miyazaki prefecture in southern Japan where Reiko grew up. He had found a position in the Ministry of Law in Tokyo. His family was eager for him to settle into a marriage with a woman from near his natal village, because they feared that as a single man in Tokyo he would be vulnerable to the conniving women of the city. Mr. Tsurumi was part of a cohort of men who became white-collar workers and made up the burgeoning urban middle class. Sons of farmers, they migrated to Tokyo to pursue higher education and to enter jobs in government and corporations. His elder brother, the family's firstborn son, remained in Kagoshima and inherited the family farm.[2]

Reiko went to see her uncle who had arranged the marriage and declared that she would not marry Mr. Tsurumi. Her uncle did not say a word. He simply rolled out a large piece of calligraphy paper in his sitting room and gave Reiko an ink brush and a big ink tablet and said, "Reiko, write down point by point why Tsurumi is a man you shouldn't marry." Reiko could not come up with a single point about what was wrong with Mr. Tsurumi himself. She had only met him once. All she knew was that she did not want to marry him. She just sat there silent, and glared at her uncle. He stated coolly that not wanting to get married was not a good enough reason to decline the marriage proposal.

The day of her wedding, Reiko cried and cried. Her younger cousins watched her with mouths agape, probably thinking that marriage was a terrible thing. Reiko wanted desperately to remain single for a few more years. Getting married meant that she could not continue her work as a culinary teacher and that she would have to leave her family in Miyazaki and move to Tokyo.

The marriage proceeded, and Reiko and her husband moved to Tokyo where they set up a household in a boarding house. They lived in a tiny five-mat *tatami* room (approximately 26.5 square feet). Each day, her husband went to work in the ministry office in Kasumigaseki while she led the life of a professional housewife.

The late 1940s, when the two started their married life, was a time of major social transformation in Japanese society. Among the many changes that were introduced was a new constitution that declared the fundamental equality of the sexes in marriage and a new civil code that officially abolished the patriarchal household system known as the *ie*. As the *ie* was abolished and people came to live primarily in nuclear families, the role of the wife gradually shifted. Instead of being a subordinate member of the extended family, taking orders from her mother-in-law and the male patriarch, she was now to be an equal partner in a dyadic relationship with her husband. She was responsible for managing the entire domestic arena so that her husband could devote all his energy to work in the public sphere. Women were entrusted with taking care of various aspects of the household including cleaning, cooking, and the family's health and hygiene.

This model of marriage, in which a husband and wife had separate and distinct spheres of responsibility, had gained the state's support from late in the nineteenth century; Christian intellectuals promoted it as progressive. It drew on the Meiji state's "good wife, wise mother" (*ryôsai kembô*) ideology, which valorized women's careers as "managers of domestic affairs in households and nurturers of children" (Uno 1993, 294). The division of labor and roles between the husband who exerted himself in his work and represented the family to wider society and the wife who managed the home is summarized in the following statement by Sakai Toshihiko, founder of the magazine, *Katei Zasshi*: "[T]he husband was to function as 'prime minister and foreign minister' while the wife was to serve as 'finance minister and home minister' responsible for the household budget, education, and hygiene" (Sakai in Ambaras 1998, 28–29). A unique feature of wives' responsibility in Japanese households was their management of domestic accounting. Women's magazines frequently featured case studies of household budgets and stories of exemplary thrifty women who allocated one-third or more of their household income to savings (Ishii and Jarkey 2002). The husband's role, meanwhile, was to exert himself fully in the workplace and bring home a pay packet. His "noninterference" in domestic matters was framed as a virtue (Fuess 2005, 275).

The early days of her marriage were marked by a series of clashes with her husband. Reiko described her husband as a very patriarchal man. One weekend, a high school friend came to visit the couple. Talking to her friend late at night when she thought her husband was asleep, Reiko said, "You should have a passionate love affair before you marry." After her friend went home, Reiko's husband grabbed her by the neck of her kimono and hurled her to the ground at the door of their apartment. He was furious. He said, "You don't know why I'm angry?" She replied, "I have no idea." To which he yelled, "I'm so disappointed to know you are a woman with such thoughts. How dare you tell a young single woman to have a passionate love affair before getting married? I had no idea. Get out of here." He pushed her into the door, leaving her with bruises all over her body. Her husband said he had never intended to marry "such a salacious woman." If she wanted to remain living in their apartment, she should lay her hand across her chest and "reflect deeply on what she had said," and never think such a thing again.

Reiko recollected how she wanted to return to her family in Kyushu, but it was so far from Tokyo, and her baby was only a toddler. Her husband believed that, as his wife, she should stay at home and obey him quietly. The couple clashed over Reiko's desire to resume Noh training at age twenty-eight after their daughter, Yaeko, had entered kindergarten. Mr. Tsurumi had been strongly opposed to Reiko resuming her training in Noh dancing and chanting, for it would entail a sizeable outlay of funds from the household budget. "None of my colleagues' wives would dream of asking their husbands to pay for such a hobby," he protested. "I'm a junior civil servant. How can I possibly afford your Noh training?"

Acquiring Certifications

Reiko took matters into her own hands. To pay for her Noh training, she asked her natal family in Miyazaki to send her money and also did some sewing at home to earn some extra income. She did not tell her husband that her family was supporting her learning because she knew he would take offense at this. The Noh master she trained with was Hayashi Tadao.[3] Twice a week, she went to his house to work as his secretary; in return, she got her training at lower cost. Her uncle, with whom she continued to communicate in writing, supported her training in Noh.

She arranged her life according to a strict schedule so that she could resume her Noh training and fit it into the life of an industrious housewife. Getting up at four each morning, she began with the laundry. Because the apartment walls in the civil servants' apartment block where she now lived were thin and the washing machine was noisy, she washed everything by hand. She then cooked the family's breakfast, prepared lunches for her husband and their daughter Yaeko, served her husband breakfast, took Yaeko to kindergarten, and went grocery shopping. She completed all these tasks by 10 a.m., so she could spend from 10 a.m. to 2:30 p.m. at her Noh classes. At 3 p.m. each day, she picked Yaeko up from kindergarten and dashed home, often dragging her by the hand. As soon as they returned home, Yaeko helped Reiko string up her apron and Reiko busied herself preparing the dinner. Sometimes Mr. Tsurumi came home early, and Yaeko would cry out, "Oh Daddy! You're home! We just got home too." Mr. Tsurumi would shoot Reiko a smirk, as if to say, "You can't fool me." He didn't say a word, but he was checking to see when she returned home. If Mr. Tsurumi had his way, he would have had a wife who was always at home.

In her late thirties, Reiko gained a *shokutaku* certification, which qualified her to take students or apprentices (*deshi*) of her own. Hayashi Sensei encouraged her to take students, to further her art. Reiko had begun to give cake-making classes in her neighborhood and asked her students casually if they would like to learn some Noh chanting and dance. They were curious about Noh and wanted to help her advance her training. As she put it, they said, "Sure. We'll learn a few songs." Eight of these women are still members of the Sumire Kai. Word spread that she was teaching Noh chanting and dance. By then, the Tsurumis were living in a civil servants' housing block in central Tokyo. More and more women in the housing unit came to learn. Some of them had heard the sound of the chanting. They were curious about the deep, resonant tones coming from the apartment. Others heard the sound of the shoulder drum floating through the windows and came to ask what they were doing. "This was how my cooking classes gradually evolved into Noh chanting and dance classes."

Over the next twenty years, Reiko continued to train in Noh and steadily increased her mastery of it, learning to sing and dance more than 150 songs of increasing complexity. Each year, she staged a performance at Hayashi Sensei's recital, which was held at the Hosho Noh Theater in Tokyo. As David Plath (1980, 3) observes, to gain a legitimate place in this world, each individual must enter into "long engagements with the cultural symbols that identify experience, and with others in society who guard the meaning of the symbols." This observation is relevant to Reiko's lifelong training in Noh, which was initiated by her uncle and carried forth through long years of training with Noh actors. In her late fifties, Reiko was awarded the license of the *jun shokubun,* the second-highest level of accreditation, in the Hosho *shite* category and formally opened her own school of Noh. Hayashi Sensei was about to die and was eager for Reiko to attain this license so that she could create a formal group of her own and carry on his legacy. Hayashi Tadao had cultivated a large following of female disciples during his career. Eight of his female students attained the professional status of *jun shokubun.*

That is how the Sumire Kai was officially created in 1986. She then became a student of the acclaimed performer, Matsumoto Shigeo, who was an Intangible Cultural Property in the *shite* category.

Reiko explained to me that her husband had little idea what she was teaching in her Noh classes. But something changed when he was in his late fifties. He went to see her performance of *Dôjôji* at the Hosho Noh Theater.

Noh plays are divided into two parts, and the central character typically appears in different forms in the first and the second part. Often the characters appear at two different periods of their lives, such as youth and old age, or sometimes life and afterlife. The process of metamorphosis is particularly vivid in certain plays, such as *Dôjôji*. The *shite* appears in the first part of the play as a dancing girl who visits *Dôjôji* Temple, where a new bell is being installed. She is looking for a priest who once promised to marry her but escaped to the temple and hid in a large bell. The girl, realizing that she has been spurned, is overcome by wrath and turns into a serpent demon in the second half of the play. The serpent demon enters the temple grounds, coils itself around the temple bell, and melts it with its fury. The play reaches its crescendo with the girl's metamorphosis into the serpent demon. The play *Dôjôji* is often treated as an emblematic piece of Buddhist misogyny that sets up priests as forces of noble, pure spirituality and women (a dancing girl transformed into a serpent) as forces of profane, bestial sexuality (Klein 1991, 291).

I believe this play can also be seen as a work that foregrounds the power of change and metamorphosis. The figure of the snake can be seen in a different, more positive light. The snake, which renews itself by shedding its skin and who gets about by slithering along the ground, is a symbol of the energy of change, and as such is "both scary and inspiring" (Owen 2008, 29). The shedding of the skin is a metaphor for the cycle of birth, life, and death of humankind. The symbolism of the snake can hence be useful for representing the little deaths that people undergo during their lives (ibid.). This dramatic metamorphosis of characters between the two acts serves, in my view, as an allegory for the transformation Mr. Tsurumi witnessed from the woman he married to the one who had grown into a Noh master.

Tsurumi Sensei continued: "My husband had been calling my Noh practice my 'hobby' until then, but something changed in his perspective. He said to me, 'I realized that you were serious about Noh.'" Mr. Tsurumi built her a Noh stage in a new apartment he had purchased with his retirement payment and became increasingly supportive of her career in Noh.

Referring to her husband, she explained:

These days my husband helps me out. When he sees I'm terribly busy preparing the common room for a class, he picks up the vacuum cleaner and cleans the apartment. My husband has changed so dramatically since the early years. I don't know what did it but he changed after he retired from his civil service post and took on a job as a marriage mediator for the local ward where we lived. He said that attending to the marital disputes of hundreds of couples, he found out that there were women who were far worse than me [chuckles].

Wagamama

Tsurumi Sensei did not have at her fingertips the specific examples of women's transgressions that made them "far worse" than she. I knew from our multiple conversations that what she described as her transgressions of wifehood were her absorption in her Noh training career, commitment to teaching her students, and frequent absence from the home on teaching trips. These were qualities that would have been venerated in a male income earner, indeed deemed necessary, but they were factors for which she had to compensate over the years. She was privately concerned about the impact of her teaching career on her family life. She explained that she had, along the way, often felt remorse. One way her family sought to explain this transgressive behavior was to speak of it as her character fault, and they invoked the term *wagamama.* To explain why she was different she said, "They say I am *wagamama.*" *Wagamama* translates as selfishness, egoism, willfulness, and disobedience. It has a strong connotation of childishness. A person who is *wagamama* is thought to be pushing her own desires and agendas without consideration for others. She would say this with a tone of repentance, as if to intimate she was going against the accepted grain of adult femininity.

"My daughter and grandchildren say I am *wagamama,*" she said. "They feel sorry for my husband and always say to him that it must be hard to be married to a woman like me. Because I have so many students and am often away from the home for days at a stretch, they think I neglect my role as a wife." She had missed crucial family events such as Father's Day celebrations and birthdays. This was a source of some grumbling among her family members. They complained that a real mother, grandmother, and wife would make herself much more available to her family than she did.

Nancy Abelmann (1997) asserts the centrality of personality in accounts of social mobility in South Korea, where her informants explain their mobility stories in terms of personal characteristics. The women she interviewed described traits such as "small-heartedness" and "irresponsibility" as reasons why they did or did not succeed in moving up the socioeconomic ladder. Abelmann remarks upon the irony that the personality traits "of which women were most critical . . . resulted in positive outcomes for their lives" (1997, 805). In the case of Tsurumi Sensei, the quality that may have facilitated her mobility was that of being *wagamama.*

While Sensei sometimes spoke with sadness about the attitudes of her family, she would chuckle about this pejorative label. I got a sneaking sense that she had come to see being *wagamama* as a good thing. "I am *wagamama!*" she would say and then erupt into a loud chuckle. "I do not follow the adage of 'when old, follow your children.'" In those moments, she seemed to have claimed *wagamama* as one of the secrets of her health in late life. When Tsurumi Sensei laughed heartily in this way, often in front of me and other students in the Noh class, she infused the term with a positive valence.

One day after class, the concept of women doing what they want came up in a discussion of gender relations. Assembled in the training room were Tsurumi Sensei, Uchida Teruyo, a fellow student, and myself. Teruyo, now in her sixties, had been widowed in her thirties and subsequently raised her son by herself while working at a girls' high school in Tokyo.

Teruyo stated, "I think women should be more assertive. They should put themselves forth as who they are. It's a pity if women hold back from expressing themselves."

Tsurumi Sensei nodded in agreement and added, "My mother was a conservative woman who was born in the late Meiji period [1868–1912] but even she used to say to me, 'Reiko-chan, women can't always be holding back. Sometimes, they have to put themselves forward and assert themselves.'" Tsurumi Sensei drew an imaginary line across the edge of the Noh stage as she quoted her mother: "'Depending on the situation, one must step back from the line or step out beyond it. You need to use your wisdom to know when to step forward.'"

She said it had taken her many years to develop this wisdom. In addition to knowing when to step forward, it was also about developing the audacity to speak out, in spite of possible censure. The nature of this censure is real, for a person becomes marked as an anomaly and must deal with that censure. For Tsurumi Sensei, learning Noh was a decision that she lived with and sustained, in spite of the hostile reaction from her husband, in the hope that, as she said, "someone would eventually understand my position."

Teruyo, who had heard Reiko recount her story, said, "This might be a little forward of me to say, but your mother lost her husband quite young. I think this allowed her to express a lot of her power. I feel the same about myself. These days, more of my peers are widows and it's so refreshing to spend time with them. It's because they are living the way they want."

I asked whether more women may want to be widows, and Teruyo replied with a chuckle: "Women have become used to having their husbands around so they probably would still rather have them alive." With a bit of consternation in her voice, Reiko responded to my comment: "Women would prefer that they have their husbands. Even with constraints, I think women would rather have their husbands alive."

Culinary Competence

Tsurumi Sensei was known among her students as a consummate cook. At each class, she served hearty meals, which she prepared from 4 a.m. on the morning of the class. She rotated the menu regularly and served seasonal delicacies, often from her hometown in Miyazaki. She brought large quantities of pickles and fruit on the plane back from her trips to southern Japan and would jokingly refer to herself as a farmer who carried an enormous basket of vegetables on her back to peddle to her city consumers. She cooked much of this food in her large kitchen.

The multitude of daytime television programs dedicated to explicating culinary techniques and teaching recipes shows that culinary competence is valued and that women, particularly of Sensei's generation, were expected to be skilled in cooking. She claimed that she loved to cook, but I dare say it was also a skill she had incorporated into her being over decades through a determined effort to develop her credentials as a housewife. Her capacity to cook and feed a crowd has imbued her with legitimacy and lays the groundwork to develop an auxiliary career teaching Noh.

Tsurumi Sensei was an intriguing figure in that she maintained her commitment to performing a housewifely role as part of her professional toolkit. Interestingly, whenever she visited Noh actors, directors of Noh theaters, and others with whom she claimed she had to maintain good working relationships for the Sumire Kai, she carried jars of homemade pickled cumquats and plums and pungent salted fish. Having sampled many of these myself, I am aware of how delectable they are. However, they are unwieldy to carry, and some are smelly. On first glance and whiff, these foods seem anomalous. They seem to reinforce her difference from these men. Moreover, bringing the whiff of the kitchen and her culinary persona into interactions with Noh actors seemed to dilute her professional standing. But as I watched Sensei over many months, I began to note that these personal homemade gifts were her way of sharing her love of cooking. They were also her way of negotiating the enormous levels of ambivalence toward women in the deeply hierarchical, patriarchal world of Noh. The way Tsurumi Sensei asserted and maintained a place in the Noh world was to tactically remain "other" within the system and to reinforce and own that difference.

Take for example the night of the gala party. Sensei and I were in a cab, heading toward the Tokyo Dome Hotel for a gathering of Noh actors and Sumire Kai members. In the cab, she opened a bag and showed me two beautifully wrapped jars of pickled kumquats and a small jar of pickled plums. "These are for Mr. Sasaki," she said with an impish grin.

Mr. Sasaki, the ninety-two-year-old director of the Yokohama Noh Theater, was a man of great health and would be giving the welcoming toast. "It's always a pleasure to meet you," she said as she presented him with the kumquats and plums. Mr. Sasaki bowed and thanked her for the gifts.

We proceeded to enter the large hall where Noh actors, members of the Sumire Kai, and others from the Noh world were seated at round tables for the gala party. Reiko and I seated ourselves with others at one of the tables. Looking around, I counted probably two hundred people in the hall.

Mr. Sasaki walked briskly to the podium and was greeted by applause. "I want to toast Tsurumi Reiko Sensei tonight," he said. "It's very rare for women to attain the heights that Tsurumi Sensei has done. She has a very large number of students not only in Tokyo but also in cities around Japan. I want to congratulate her for her accomplishments." Raising his sake cup, he said "*Campai!*" (Cheers!) The assembled guests raised their sake cups, "*Campai!*" Mr. Sasaki continued. "I may also add that Tsurumi Sensei is very masculine. She is very assertive. But fortunately, she has some womanly parts to her too," he said. "Today, she gave me a number of prized delicacies: vinegared kumquats and pickled plums."

I looked sideways at Sensei to register her reaction to Mr. Sasaki's congratulatory address. Thinking she may have taken some offense at his comment, I searched her face for some indication of irritation. But she looked unperturbed. Her hands on her lap, her back straight, and her shoulders relaxed, she gazed straight at Mr. Sasaki who continued to speak.

"I wish to designate Tsurumi Sensei an excellent role model for the younger generation of women in Japan today, many of whom don't know how to cook. And, even worse, they are choosing to postpone marriage and childbirth. *Campai!*" The room broke into applause and Mr. Sasaki walked off the stage.

Later that evening, when Sensei and I returned to the Sumire Kai training center, I broached the subject of Mr. Sasaki's speech and asked her what she thought of his statement. She responded, "Moore-san, Japanese men and women are said to be equal. But I discovered there are some things that women are expected to be able to do, and things that men are expected to do. Especially for women of my generation, being a good cook is considered very important. I decided to excel in the arts of femininity in addition to pursuing Noh. Besides, I found out long ago that there are many benefits in being an excellent cook." By assiduously creating the identity of a Noh teacher who cooks delicious meals, and at times engaging in what Mora Lloyd (1999) calls a hyperbolic performance of womanhood by serving elaborate meals and delicacies to her students, husband, and male colleagues in the Noh world, she was able to guard her career in the Noh arts, a field she frequently called a "man's world."

Retaining the housewife identity was central to her personal politics. Tsurumi Sensei strategically deployed idioms of the housewife as part of her pedagogical toolkit. Her approach to thriving in the male-dominated world of Noh was to actively construct or even exaggerate her female social identity.

Conclusion

Tsurumi Sensei's life story is at once unique and exemplary of a broader social phenomenon in postwar Japan where increasing numbers of women learned Noh. As stated earlier, in 1948 the performer Tsumura Kimiko became one of five women to enter the Noh Council, and was recognized as a professional performer by the Kanze school of Noh. Meanwhile, the Noh schools packaged their received knowledge and marketed their traditions to a new demographic of amateur students, which included housewives such as Tsurumi. She came of age in a historical period when the life of the professional housewife, who dedicates herself to managing the home, gained ascendancy as an idealized way of life. We see how Tsurumi Sensei embraced this role but also found it confining and turned to Noh training as a way to construct an identity independent of her housewife role and to become a master teacher in late life.

Pivotal to her life was an early encounter with her maternal uncle who taught her Noh songs in the fields near a rice paddy in southern Japan during the World War II. He was a force that ignited her commitment to Noh training and to the transmission of this art form today. Her commitment can be seen in the seriousness with which she taught the students in the temple. The dislocations of the war created an unexpectedly close relationship between a middle-aged man and a young woman coming of age. Her uncle's loss of all of the markers of social identity except the cultural capital of Noh placed a special urgency on his effort to transmit this art. His message about polishing *gei* amidst the vicissitudes of life became a compass for Sensei throughout her life:

> As you sing and polish your *gei* over time, it will shine from within. Sing, dear girl, sing. Your *gei* will shine through. Polish it, for it is something that nothing, and nobody, can take away from you.

A major theme in this chapter is the transition from the prewar world to the postwar one. Part of what gives cultural authenticity to a person such as Tsurumi is that she has experienced the world before 1945. She represents a time when Japan was most united, when values were clear-cut, where there was not the ambiguity between the sexes as there is right now. Her uncle was displaced from the city, during a liminal period when many people were displaced from their familiar worlds. Within that bounded-off, timeless, period and place she was initiated into Noh practice. Her teacher was an older male, providing her with a particular authentication. At the time, she felt his training was bothersome, but as she looks back on it she represents it as an initiation. It is as if her entire destiny was prefigured in that field beside the rice paddy.

Moreover, a powerful series of cultural symbols has assembled around her. The discipline and hardship she experienced in wartime give her authority to yell at others sixty years later, and her story of hardship in her youth becomes a justification for her departing from the housewife role. We see a cultural logic in the way her life has unfolded.

The next chapter describes the rituals of learning in the Noh class. We will see Tsurumi's lifelong discipline manifesting in her classroom, giving a sense of order and structure to her life and to others'. Asked what matters to them as they grow older, the women articulate two items of paramount significance: social community and opportunity for self-actualization. The Noh class provides both.

Notes

1. Columbia Music Entertainment. 2002. *Yokyoku* (Noh song). Online. Available: http://jtrad.columbia.jp/eng/n_yokyoku.html; accessed Aug., 12, 2013.

2. See Vogel (1973, 93) for more discussion of the way households in rural areas reproduced themselves in the postwar period by retaining the eldest son while sending younger siblings to urban areas.

3. Hayashi Tadao is a pseudonym.

3

Rituals of Learning

Tsurumi Sensei offers instruction in Tokyo on Thursdays, Fridays, and Saturdays. On these days, she opens the doors of her Noh classroom at 9 a.m. and keeps them open until the final student leaves around 6 p.m. Among the students who come are housewives, schoolteachers, business professionals, judges, dentists, some university students, and small children. At the Sumire Kai, the schedule is demanding, because of the group's particular approach in which students eat the same meals and watch each other's training over eight hours. Students learn a lot from watching each other. This educational leisure activity serves as a pathway for self-actualization for these women. Learning in the Sumire Kai often feels harrowing because of the intensity of Sensei's teaching. She conveys the expectation that all students will reach new heights through continuing practice.

Pedagogy of Dread

Upon arriving at the Sumire Kai training center, the women assemble their bags in a back corner of the room, change from their dresses and suits into loose-fitting pants. The women seat themselves in two rows on floor cushions and place their Noh songbooks, recording devices, and pencils on small tables (*kendai*). They typically chat quietly for a few moments until Tsurumi Sensei arrives and seats herself in one corner of the room. Then the day's *keiko* begins. The room holds an air of solemnity.

Tsurumi Sensei calls out to one of the women and asks her to start her dance. The student, a woman aged about sixty, and comfortably attired in a loose-fitting shirt and comfortably fitting slacks and wearing white *tabi* (socks) walks onto the stage and takes her position in front of a representation of a green pine tree. After she sings the opening line of a play, the rest of the students, who are the chorus, break into song. Powered by their deep, resonant voices, the student quietly moves into her dance sequence. She does the gliding steps of Noh dance called the *suri-ashi*. The *suri-ashi* consists of a slow, highly controlled motion that involves sliding the feet in alternating sequences across the stage. Each step involves a careful shift of body weight from one foot to the other; one leg is slightly bent and holds the weight while the other one is kept straight. The student has been instructed by the teacher to move her legs imagining that her legs extend from her navel. In her right hand, she holds a fan. She moves from one section of the stage to the next, doing the glide, circular motions, and occasional hard stamps of the feet.

As Loic Wacquant says of the boxer's training, training in Noh dance is an unfolding journey of discovery across the expanses of the dancer's corporeality (1995, 511). Through endless repetition of the same movements of the Noh glide and the fan maneuver, the dancer learns to work with and feel the working of different muscles within her thighs, hips, and abdomen. She tries to expand her body's powers of smooth motion, so that a movement that initially feels like a robotic and wooden walk increasingly becomes a fluid motion of feet moving smoothly across the stage. When dancing, she maintains a straight alignment of her nose, navel, and groin, so that her torso appears to be perfectly still, even as she is moving steadily. In Noh, the dancer must remain completely centered, storing an immense concentration of energy (*ki*) within her body

(Yamanaka 2008, 79). As Helena Wulff (1998, 8) says of the distinction in ballet between the acts of watching and doing, watching Noh is quite different from becoming a student of it. The latter entails subjecting the self to the discipline of learning.

In Noh dance, the dancer embodies form (*kata*). The kata have developed over many centuries and can be "reinterpreted somewhat, but they are seldom blatantly broken" (Brazell 1998, 124). As Brazell observes, the creativity of Noh performance is expressed through the "how" of performance, that is, the life that the performer breathes into the forms she has received from her teachers (ibid.). *Kata* are acquired through *keiko*. The direct transmission of *kata* from Noh teacher to student is pivotal in the acquisition of *kata*. Dancers learn Noh by modeling

Figure 3.1. Tsurumi Sensei Teaching Noh Dance. Photograph by Katrina L. Moore.

the teacher's movements. This relationship provides the basis for students to develop a somatosensory awareness of *kata* (Fraleigh 2000, 57). In Noh practice, learning with the body takes precedence over the study of dance texts. Dancers acquire skill through observations of the teacher's movements. The relationship between teacher and student can last for decades and is generally exclusive. Most Noh students learn from one, or possibly two, Noh teachers in the course of their lifetime.

Takayama Setsuko, aged seventy, is a student who is frequently corrected by Tsurumi Sensei. As a senior student, she has been attending classes for many years but continues to make mistakes. When Setsuko makes a series of wrong dance moves one after another, Tsurumi Sensei becomes angry and pauses the dancing. She begins to hurl her comments at Setsuko. "Why haven't you made any progress? Why don't you learn anything I've taught you? This is terrible." Sensei continues yelling for a few minutes.

The first time I hear this tirade is my second day of class at the Sumire Kai. I am at the doorway of the training center about to enter when I hear Sensei showering her criticisms onto the student. Being new to the group, I am taken aback by the intensity of the yelling and imagine what it would be like to be the target of Tsurumi's admonitions.

From inside the room, I can hear Sensei interrogating Setsuko. "You haven't been practicing, have you?" A silence follows. Then Sensei's voice erupts again, "I've taught you this so many times and you still don't get it." Another silence follows, at which point I decide to let myself in. I open the sliding door and expect that Sensei will pause her scolding, but she continues to yell at Setsuko, barely acknowledging that I have walked into the room. The rest of the women sit quietly, appearing quite calm. Finally, Setsuko blurts out, "Excuse me, Sensei. Please excuse me." I later ask Setsuko what keeps her coming back to the

Sumire Kai. She explains, "This training is tough, but no matter how much Sensei yells at me, I still feel glad that I came to class. I can take her criticisms because I know they're not personal."

In fact, a common theme in Japanese narratives of apprenticeships is that of cruel tutelage (Bestor 2004; Kondo 1990; de Vos and Wagatsuma 1978). Skills are transmitted through a mode of training that is anything but gentle. Thus, the fierceness in Sensei's teaching should not come as a surprise for those familiar with apprenticeships in various Japanese applied and traditional performing arts.

Sensei uses a gentler tone for those she perceives to be diligent but lacking in feeling. She is still impassioned. When students have done the moves correctly but their performance is mechanical and lacks vibrancy, she cries out, "Where is your soul (*tamashii*)? Don't you know you have to put your *feeling* into your practice? You are too preoccupied with simply copying form." One student, Minako, is practicing a dance segment from the play called *Matsukaze*. As *Matsukaze,* she is holding the hunting robe of her lover, Ariwara no Yukihira, and pines for his return. A very fastidious student, Minako asks Sensei, "Shall I hold the robe this high? Shall I hold the robe up this way?" Because Minako poses these questions at a time when they are approaching the recital, Sensei is even more annoyed. She replies, "Once you are on stage at the final recital, you will not feel emotion, but during training, I want you to try your best to feel the feeling in the play." Minako still does not understand this. Finally, Sensei gets up from her chair and moves swiftly toward Minako. Squeezing Minako's body toward her, Sensei says, "Imagine you are holding your lover! Imagine what it's like to hold your lover! You must feel, Minako-san. You must FEEL." Minako, a little stunned by the hug, smiles and says, "Okay, Sensei. I get it."

On other occasions, she says, in a manner reminiscent of her uncle's story of polishing *gei,* discussed in the last chapter:

"As a woman you can wear beautiful clothes, bedeck yourself with jewels, and spend hours doing your makeup. But when all that is taken away and you are naked you must have something that will make you shine from within. That is what *gei* is."

Learning to Chant

Students also learn to chant at the Sumire Kai. A noteworthy feature of the teaching of Noh chanting is its reliance on direct oral transmission. The teacher engages with each student individually to ensure that the student acquires the correct melody (*fushi*). When teaching chanting, teachers instruct students to carefully imitate the curl of the lips and to repeat after them, clearly enunciating the tones. This mode of mimicking the teacher is colloquially called "parrot return." The student literally returns or repeats the words stated by the teacher.

A student called Masumi remembered distinctly her first lesson with Tsurumi Sensei. Tsurumi Sensei asked Masumi to sit down on the floor across from her and gave her the *Crane and Tortoise* songbook. "In the first class, I was asked to sing—just like that. We did not do any vocalizing to warm up. The teacher then simply said shout. She said, 'You probably have never shouted like this, but please shout with a loud voice.'" Tsurumi Sensei and Masumi went through the song line by line, for a total of three times.

> How numerous the examples of things that last a
> thousand ages.
> How numerous the examples of things that last a
> thousand ages.
> What should we begin with?
> First, the tortoise, green as the small Princess Pine.

Masumi continued,

Before I opened my own mouth, I thought *utai* sounded like a Buddhist chant. But when I started doing *utai,* I thought "this is really interesting." I was so captivated. It's actually very pleasurable to sing *utai*.

I realized that it's really important to do *keiko*. Until I did *keiko*, Noh seemed so boring. I couldn't figure out what was interesting about it. When I experienced it physically, it became very interesting.

Another woman, Koike Takako, recalled a day about six months into her own training with Tsurumi Sensei.

I sat in front of her, with my feet tucked beneath my legs *seiza* style and my Noh songbook placed in front of me. Tsurumi Sensei sat facing me on a low chair with her back straight, her mouth open wide, and her gaze never leaving my face. I was in the midst of learning to sing my second Noh song, *Momijigari*. My hands were clammy with perspiration. Next to me were fellow students who were silent, watching the pedagogy unfold. Tsurumi Sensei drew a line with her fan in the air, as if to lead my voice along with it. "Follow the movement of my fan, Koike-san." I faltered. Tsurumi Sensei glared at me. "Sing, Koike-san. Now!" We sang the first three lines of the *kiri* section of the song in unison.

Eventually, Takako tuned into her own chanting and her breathing. She could feel her voice becoming more powerful and more clear. The sound of her voice gradually came to hold its own.

Speaking of this type of training, where a teacher will yell at one student in front of others, one woman states, "When it is time for me to take my turn in front of my fellow students, I often ask myself, *why* am I doing this? But I can stand it because I think of the final goal." The final goal she is referring to is the performance on the stage. She feels she can endure the challenges of the pedagogy because they prepare her for that moment. She also feels that Tsurumi Sensei's assessment is very clear and fair: "Even if learning is far from enjoyable or relaxing, I'm comfortable in her classroom. I'm assessed appropriately for what I've done: praised for what I've done well, scolded for what I have not learned."

Noh learning is also generally a long-term undertaking. The respect conferred on amateurs who have refined their Noh practice over decades establishes that learning as an aspirational goal. The most experienced members of the group, who have more than thirty years experience at the center and have learned over 150 plays, are highly regarded by the more junior women. They encourage the younger women and also establish a distinction in status, in terms of skill, over those who are new at the training center. This hierarchy of skill, often though not necessarily correlated with years of experience, exists in other traditional arts, which accord respect to those who have been studying these arts for longer (de Coker 1998, 3–74).

When I was preparing for my first performance on the Noh stage and was trying desperately to master my first dance performance, a long-timer at the center, Ryoko, age sixty-eight, observed wisely: "You can't try to immediately become something that has taken [us] years and years to embody. It takes years and years of constant refinement. There are things you are capable of now; there are things you will be able to do after two years of training, and there are things you will be able to do after five years of training." As a rather eager learner of Noh who had been coming to extra practice sessions in preparation for my debut recital, I replied, "If only I could become as good as you when I am in my seventies." Momoko, another student, age seventy-two, who had been training for thirty years, said, "Remember, it's your first performance. People will applaud you for that. If you try to imitate those who have been doing it for longer, it will be odd." Possibly sensing my gloom, Momoko added, with a bit more sympathy: "At least, your posture is excellent. You are moving very confidently. That is good."

Lunchtime Camaraderie

When lunch hour approaches, some of the students stop practice early and go down to the common room, located in another apartment on the second floor of the building. They prepare the meal while Tsurumi Sensei continues to teach students to dance and chant. Through an intercom, the students announce when lunch is ready, and the others, including Sensei, go downstairs. Sensei puts on her apron to oversee the final preparations of the food that she began cooking at four that morning. Suddenly, she is no longer the harsh pedagogue. Lunch provides a break from the intensity of the learning. Sensei serves delicacies from her hometown of Aoshima in Miyazaki prefecture, such as fresh oysters, a special grilled chicken called Miyazaki *jidori,* and Miyazaki's famous citrus fruit (*hyûga natsu mikan*). These meals are included in the students' lesson fees. She keeps entering the room with new servings of food, urging students to eat more.

Once she has finished serving, she sits down at the table. Usually, Sensei becomes the center of the conversation in these discussions. She sometimes tells a story about herself in a teasing way. For example, one day she said, "My husband has given me a new name. I'm out so often, he calls me Walkabout Pig (*dearukiton*)." She continues, "When I get home and he wants to tell me something, I fall asleep exhausted so he calls me Sleepy Pig (*gûtara-ton*)." Tomiko, sitting across from Sensei and laughing, says, "There has to be a third one. Things like this always come in threes." Sensei thinks for a while and says, "Oh yes. In the mornings, as soon as I finish my breakfast, I'm on the phone to people so my husband calls me Telephone Pig (*den-ton*)."

The strict pedagogy resumes after lunch.

Fees

The total cost for a year of Noh *keiko* varies. The monthly fee for *keiko* varies for each person and is based on a sliding scale. For instance, when I studied Noh dance and chanting at the Sumire Kai, I was a student and I paid five thousand yen ($55) per month for my classes. Other students paid considerably higher fees (approximately $220 per month) because of their higher incomes.

In addition, students purchase the Sumire Kai uniform, a deep violet–hued set of kimono and *hakama* (a pleated skirt worn over kimono that go out in an A-line), which they wear offstage on the days of the recital. They also buy inner garments to wear inside the stage costumes, and a shoulder drum. The cost of performing in the large biennial recital ranges anywhere from $2,200 for a short dance sequence to $17,000 for a full Noh performance. The cost is higher than for the recitals staged in Tsurumi Sensei's home because of the fees that are paid to the hereditary head of the Noh school, the *iemoto*, and to Noh actors who provide the musical accompaniment to the students' performances. As the cost of the classes, costumes, and instruments reveals, membership in the Sumire Kai requires a significant degree of financial commitment. Given that the average monthly income for Japanese in their sixties is $4,600 and for Japanese in their seventies slightly lower at $4,230, the cost of Noh classes and performance would be out of reach of most Japanese senior citizens.[1]

Recitals

The Sumire Kai holds a recital each year in the city of Miyazaki in southern Japan. For this recital, Sumire Kai members gather from the cities of Tokyo, Kōfu, Fuj-Yoshida, Fukuoka, Miyazaki, Kumamoto, and Kagoshima gather. On the days before and after the recital, they take sightseeing trips to castles and burial mounds on the outskirts of Miyazaki City, and visit restaurants to savor local delicacies. It was during one of these trips that I came to appreciate the important role recitals and trips play in deepening amateurs' identification with their leisure activity. Over the course of three days, the students take part in various activities that shift from performing, to dining, sleeping, bathing, singing, sightseeing, and traveling. By sharing the same meals, the same rooms, and the same thrills and angst of performing onstage, students develop a shared identity as members of the Sumire Kai. Emile Durkheim's notion of "effervescence" captures the effects of this coming together through the recital (Durkheim 1995). Effervescence arises when human beings feel themselves transformed, and are in fact transformed, through ritual. They experience the agent of transformation as external to themselves, but this force is created by the fact of "assembling and temporarily living a collective life that transports individuals beyond themselves" (Fields 1995, xii). Participants experience themselves as "grander than at ordinary times" (Fields 1995, xli). The three days of intense interaction at the Sumire Kai recital become the basis for students to set aside their day-to-day lives and deepen their commitment to this performing art.

In preparation for their performances, some of the students share their thoughts with me about the plays they will perform on the Noh stage. Mariko, a sixty-year-old author, is to perform the celestial being in the play *Hagoromo* (Feathered Robe). The story originally derives from a Chinese tale in which a fisherman finds the robe of a young maiden from the heavens and will not give it back to her. He makes her his wife and they live together for many years and have children until one day he allows her to leave and she returns to the heavens. The Noh version is different: the fisherman discovers the robe of the heavenly being while she is bathing and decides to keep it as a "treasure for all future generations" (Yasuda 1989, 45). When the heavenly being emerges from the spring and demands that he give back her robe—actually her wings—he initially refuses. The fisherman eventually begins to acquiesce as he considers the prospect of being able to watch her mesmerizing dance, but he is still reluctant to return her robe, imagining she will take flight the moment he returns it to her. She persuades him that she will keep her word. "There is no deceit in heaven," she declares. "I shall only fly away *after* I dance." Eventually, the fisherman relents and returns the robe. Donning the robe, she dances a resplendent dance; once she finishes, she flies away into the clouds and to her home in the heavens.

"I imagine myself to be this celestial being who carries the message that there is no deceit in this world," says Mariko. "The play is far removed from the everyday life of human beings where people do not keep their word, but it's why I like this play, because it reminds me of a higher place of morality." By enacting the characters from Noh plays, women experience a scope of fantasy and depth of emotion they feel they do not otherwise have.

The morning of the recital, the backstage of the theater is abuzz with activity. Women in deep violet–hued robes bustle about, helping those who are about to perform put on their costumes. The costumes consist of multiple layers: two undergarments, a kimono that comes down to the calf, a string to tie the *kimono, hakama,* an *obi* (a broad sash worn with *hakama)*, and a string to complete the costume. Putting on all the layers of the costume takes a full half-hour and involves quite a bit of yanking and pulling.

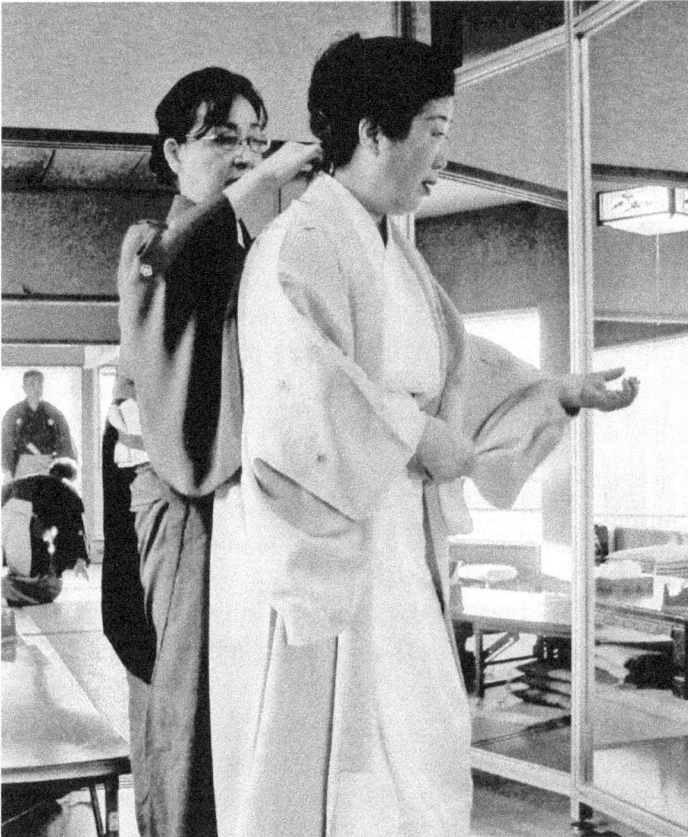

Figure 3.2. Students Preparing for a Performance. Photograph by Katrina L. Moore.

As students await their turn, some find a space backstage and go through their dance repertoire several times. When it is nearing their turn to dance, the chorus members first enter the stage and seat themselves at the back of the stage. The performer follows. She slowly walks toward the center of the stage and takes her position in front of the representation of the large green pine tree. After she sings the opening line of a play, the chorus breaks into song. Powered by their chanting, the performer quietly moves through her dance sequence. The performance is usually brief, but if it is done well, and if her performance shows a concentration and grace that captivate the audience, it can transform the space of the stage into an exquisite moment where the flow of time seems to dissolve. The only thing that matters in that room at that moment is the masterful glide of the dancer's body. After the performance, other members of the Sumire Kai go up to the performer and congratulate her, bowing deeply and offering comments on the dance.

At the recital, one of the highlights was a performance of the play *Izutsu* (The Well Cradle), by Koike Takako. After her performance, I congratulated Takako. She smiled and replied, "Now that I've reached this level Tsurumi Sensei will push me to the next. There is never a point of completion or perfection." Takako's words illuminate one of the key aspects of the learning process of the traditional performing arts, where even after decades of training, students believe that mastery is unattainable and there is yet much more to learn.

The evening after a recital, many of the Sumire Kai members make their way from their hotel rooms to the communal bath located at the hotel where they are staying. There, they relax and soak their aching bodies in the hot springs. Bathing in the large bathtub with fellow students is a way of unwinding after a long day of performance. It is an opportunity to share the tales of hardship around the recital and to laugh about the fear that Sensei has inspired in the weeks leading up to the recital.

The official policy of the Sumire Kai is that students may not socialize outside of the class; Tsurumi Sensei believes that it disturbs the dynamics of the classroom. She is quite adamant about this point. However, students from different regional groups stay in contact. Many students secretly meet with each other. They have developed friendships outside of class.

Mud Swamp

A final element worth considering about amateur Noh practice is the cost of participating. As I described earlier in the chapter, the traditional arts can be costly. Given the unique way that amateur Noh learning is structured, where students are expected to enter into a close relationship with one teacher and to commit themselves fully to that teacher's teaching style, some find it burdensome. Such commitment entails a growing immersion in the group's activities, including regular participation in recitals. Students may have to buy tickets to their teacher's performances. In certain cases, they need to pay for their teacher's costumes for their stage performances as well.

I occasionally met people who found the financial outlays too constraining. Tachibana Sayuri, a former student of Noh dance and chanting, was one person who stopped. She claimed she would never return, saying that learning Noh was akin to entering a "mud swamp." Sayuri and I met over lunch, and she filled me in on the details of her life. She was in her fifties, married, with two grown sons.

> I pursued Noh training for many years from when I was a teenager. My parents did Noh training and my sister did too. I continued it until I had my two boys, and even wrote my master's thesis and some chapters on Noh. But I stopped when my younger son became very ill. After I stopped, I didn't go back. I have no desire to resume Noh training.

She continued,

> The world of the traditional arts is like a *mud swamp*. As one gets sucked in, it's hard to come out. There are recitals each spring and each autumn that teachers

encourage students to participate in. Teachers rarely
disclose their fee structures even to their own students,
so a learner has to have a considerable degree of
financial wealth at their disposal. Some of those recitals
cost over one million yen. A lot of people don't want
to participate in the recitals because they cost a lot of
money, but when the teacher says "you must," they
can't refuse.

Sayuri paused a moment and continued,

It was awkward for me to stop going to Noh classes,
but my son was so ill that I could legitimately
withdraw from lessons without causing too much of
a storm. I have not returned since.

As I listened to Sayuri, I thought of the "culture centers"
dotted all over metropolitan centers in Japan; these centers also
give Noh lessons. I mentioned to her that these centers are far
more transparent about the cost of lessons and offer these lessons
at a more affordable fee. (I had investigated the cost of Noh
lessons at a NHK Culture Center in Tokyo and found that each
session cost about thirty-three dollars. One of their selling points
is indeed the affordability of these lessons and their avoidance of
the ritual of students giving summer and winter gifts.)
Sayuri replied,

Culture centers provide an easy route for students
to become acquainted with Noh. They provide a
framework of clear fees and schedules. The people
who join have probably seen Noh but have never
learned to chant or dance. They are curious about this
rarefied art form. But you should know that culture
centers are also venues for teachers to sift through
the students to identify those who can pay. At the

end of a term, they encourage these people to transfer to private lessons. The same applies to workplace Noh recreation groups which proliferated in Japanese companies in the high growth economic period. At the workplace, individuals pay tuition as a group. The eager ones seek out the teacher independently for private lessons. The teacher assesses whether or not to take on a student based partly on their ability to pay. Teachers favor good patrons who can pay a lot of money as gifts of gratitude for transmitting the valuable techniques.

Sayuri daintily slipped another piece of fish into her mouth and looked at me. She observed:

This world caters to those who have money. It also means that younger people who cannot afford the fees associated with participating in recitals or other older people who cannot afford to pay for Noh classes end up not learning this performing art.

Indeed, the expense associated with Noh is one of the reasons why more people are not able to experience Noh. Given the fact that students are effectively subsidizing the livelihood of Noh actors, it is difficult for younger people who have less income to do Noh. It is not economically sustainable for students to learn Noh, and some end up quitting, in spite of the fact they continue to appreciate and enjoy the physical experiences of Noh chanting and dance.

Conclusion

This chapter has explored the rituals of learning in the Sumire Kai Noh singing and dance class. Women gather to receive intensive physical and vocal training. By engaging in this training, women catapult themselves into a new world. The disciplines of learning, the close pedagogic relationship with the Noh teacher, and the performances at recitals create opportunities for women to imagine another self and to develop a sense of identity based on membership in a world of shared learning.

Note

1. Japan Statistics Bureau. Family Income and Expenditure Survey. Online. Available http://www.stat.go.jp/english/data/kakei/ct2010.htm; accessed August 12, 2013.

4

Peeling Away of Identity

The pinnacle of this training is the hour-long performance in full costume at the Noh Theater. Yet, for many women it is not simply the experience of performing at the Noh Theater that is rewarding and appealing, but also developments in states of self that arise through this training. To understand what compels these women, and their devotion of hundreds of hours to training to chant, dance, and drum, I delve into student testimonials about the experience of learning. I explore these activities' corporeal effects at a deeper level in this chapter. In particular, I explore the processes of identity formation and dissolution and the state of no-mind (*mushin*) that arises from practicing Noh. These experiential states, in turn, have important benefits on the everyday lives of these amateur women practitioners. The chapter also discusses the benefits associated with Noh in later life.

Student Testimonials on the Peeling Away of Identity

In general, the Noh class was a venue where women did not disclose details of their personal lives. It was only in our meetings outside of class that they became more open. The first occasion on which I developed a close rapport with students of the Sumire Kai was the annual recital held in the city of Miyazaki in southern Japan. Students subsequently came to share more of their observations about what led them to devote hours to this practice. Their stories include insights into their gender and career identities.

Changing Gender Identity

Michiyo, a woman in her early fifties, is an executive in a hotel chain. She began learning Noh at age fifty. She describes turning fifty as a "turning point" in her life. Her husband had a debilitating illness and he could not work, so she was the family income earner. For many years, she had lived thinking about how best to support his needs, but now she began to think she had to develop her own interests.

> At age fifty, I began to think, "I need to turn my gaze toward my own life." I wanted to look after myself [*jibun o daiji ni shitakatta*].

For Michiyo, participating in the Noh classes, and learning the techniques of dancing and chanting, contributed to a changing personal self, which was distinct from her career identity and her identity as the family income earner.

She also described her experience of turning fifty as involving a transition in her sexual identity; it was a time when her femininity was shifting. This was partly because she had experienced menopause at that age. When young, she was very conscious of constructing her identity in ways that would accentuate her femininity. She would explicitly highlight the female features of her physique by wearing tightly fitting dresses and high heels, for example, but this impulse had changed with age. In her view, the performance of femininity was a manifestation of a heteronormative desire to be acknowledged as a woman by men. In later life, she was exploring new ways in which to express her sexuality. In Noh, she found enjoyment in discovering ways in which she could be androgynous. She could experiment with enacting female and male roles. Learning to express her gender on the Noh stage seemed to her to be a good compass for how she was exploring a new performance of sexuality. Yet as we see from Noh actors' observations, the performance of femininity and masculinity in Noh is very subtle and is not about putting on exaggerated performances of the feminine and masculine. Everything happens through *kata*. As the Noh actor Uzawa Hisa explains: "Sexual difference does not matter to Noh expression" (Aoki 2012, 6). Even when women perform female roles, they do not focus on the fact that they are women themselves. They try to represent the role only through formal *kata*. As Senda Rihō, the Komparu school female performer, also says, "Each role is expressed through *kata*. I do not think about becoming the male role or female role" (Aoki 2012, 5).

Referring to the importance of *kata* for expressing gender identity in Noh performance, Michiyo says: "There are many codes. One cannot simply improvise the role as one wishes. That is, however, what is really interesting about the expression of gender in Noh."

Shedding Status with Identity

Ozawa Hiromi, age sixty-three, articulates her perspective on learning Noh. She took up Noh practice in her fifties as she was making the transition from a career as a school principal into a new job as an adjunct professor at a teacher's college. She shared her perspective on the pedagogy in the classroom:

> Learning from Tsurumi Sensei is daunting. We have to let go of any sense of security that comes from the identity we have in everyday life. Once we step inside the doorway of the *keikoba* (Noh training room), Sensei treats us all the same: as students who are there to learn Noh.

In Sensei's class, it does not matter whether someone is a business executive or famous novelist or homemaker. People's identities are respected, but they are put aside in the service of immersion in the learning.

> The fact that I was a school principal means little in this group. Sure, most people know that that was my profession. But within the class I completely let go of a sense of self I gain from my public identity. This practice of letting go is really precious. It feeds back into my current job as a college teacher. When I stand at the podium on the college campus and lecture to the students, I ask myself, "What is my foundation for engaging with my students? Is it based on my position in the hierarchy and the fact I've had a forty-year career? Or is it based on my capacity to relate to my students in a meaningful way?"

Hiromi believes that to have any credibility with her own students, she needs to be continually open to learning herself. "How do I do that? I go to the Sumire Kai. Learning things from scratch imposes humility, and the class creates an environment where I'm able to reflect on myself. I see a different self. This is really valuable to me."

She continues:

> With age, I have come to occupy a high position in the social hierarchy. I have gained more authority. But I need to be very vigilant. Seniority carries risks of hubris and arrogance. Older people can become bossy and dogmatic, especially when guiding younger generations.

She says the Noh training helps her temper these tendencies because it requires that she position herself as a learner who is learning things from scratch. Noh training is demanding for Hiromi, especially because Tsurumi scolds her for not practicing. But she claims it is a positive experience because it is humbling and it makes her realize she still has a lot to learn and improve. Hiromi smiles sheepishly. "It's kind of refreshing actually. There aren't many occasions at my age where people scold me anymore."

Letting Go

Would it not be threatening to have to shed one's identity in this way? From my observations of these rituals of learning, this practice of letting go of identity is possible because the women understand Sensei's agenda: to focus on opening students up to Noh. People's identities are respected, but they are put aside in the service of immersion in learning to dance and chant. Tsurumi Sensei provides what Donald Winnicott (1991) calls a "holding environment." This is a space in which the dissolution of identity is possible. In Winnicott's analysis, this holding environment allows for states of simply being, where identity can be suspended in creative play and in the absorbed exploration of potential (1991, 53–64). This potential emerges through relation: relation between student and teacher, student and student, and student and stage. The space is potential space because it holds possibilities, without seeking to fix people into roles or identities. In this space, potential can unfold in creative ways (Metcalfe and Game 2007, 7). When women are in this holding environment, which extends beyond the classroom to their homes, they settle into a ritual of practicing their chanting and dance. What the pedagogical relationship does is dissolve the self-consciousness that permeates identity states, allowing students', and teachers', potential to unfold (see Game and Metcalfe 2008, 4; see also Merleau-Ponty 1968, 57).

No-mind

To further illustrate the development in states of self, I analyze in particular the experiences of Hamada Emiko. Hamada Emiko and I engaged in multiple conversations in and outside class about the meaning of Noh learning to her life. Her quest to find meaning in Noh—and in particular her effort to create a space for her own self-cultivation in later life—is emblematic of the aspirations of some of the full-time homemakers in the Sumire Kai who sought through Noh to create an independent lifeworld distinct from their lives as mothers. In the process, they have developed some distance from the feelings of responsibility they had toward their children and their husbands, and from their attachment to their identities as mothers.

Hamada Emiko had been a member of the Sumire Kai for five years when I met her. She was a graceful, skillful dancer. Emiko described her encounter with Noh as one of stepping into a world that was "deep and rich." There was a sense of awe in her voice as she described this experience. Unlike Tsurumi Sensei who had been practicing Noh since she was a teenager, Emiko had little experience with it before joining the Sumire Kai at age fifty-five. She had been to the Noh Theater two or three times in her life, but that was all.

One day, I met Emiko at the Sumire Kai training site where she was practicing her dance for the autumn recital. We were the only two people there that morning. I watched Emiko on the stage, her body tipped forward in a front-leaning posture with a perfectly straight back, and her arms held out on either side of her body. A concentrated energy in her shoulder blades kept her shoulders firmly lowered. Emiko's face and torso were completely steady as she circled around the stage, the only motion coming from her legs that moved steadily forward and from the occasional sweep of her fan. After a few minutes, she completed her dance and walked off the stage. I asked her to describe the experience of dance. She spoke slowly, emphatically, articulating each word:

> When I train in Noh dance, there are times I can experience *mushin* [no-mind]. I am conscious of my body but my mind is quiet. This is the first and most important thing.

Emiko claimed that she experienced a state of *mushin,* when her breathing was deep and regular and her body had acquired knowledge of *kata* so that it could flow through a whole dance sequence. For dancers, this state of *mushin* usually arises after repeated training in the practice of performing techniques.

The state of *mushin* that Emiko experiences can be understood through what Mihaly Csikszentmihalyi has described as flow, an experience of focused awareness (1991, 65). Flow occurs when thoughts, intentions, feelings, and all the senses are focused on the present. It arises when the attainment of skill combines with a sense of ease. The claim is that when a person is in a state of flow, there is a sensation of deep, focused involvement in the activity. There is sometimes an alteration in their sense of time; hours seem to pass by in minutes, and minutes seem to stretch out to feel like hours. Importantly, there is disappearance of consciousness of egoic self. When that consciousness of egoic self disappears, people are freed from preoccupation with themselves, and they have a chance to expand the concept of who they are.

Csikszentmihalyi explains that being in a state of flow does not mean that the person is unaware of what is happening in the body. In fact, the opposite is true. The optimal experience of flow generally involves a heightened awareness of the body. A Noh dancer in a state of *mushin* is extremely aware of every movement of the body, as well as of the sound emanating from her voice as she chants. She is aware and infinitely responsive, but importantly, she is no longer in a state of being where the everyday self seeks to be in control.

Emiko spoke to me about the effects of Noh training on her life. She claimed that whenever she is "firmly present to my own sensory experience of the dance," her mind becomes more quiet, and a sense of stillness prevails. The mind that is judging and analyzing the details of everyday life becomes more still. She felt that the benefits of her practice permeated into other parts of her life. Through her Noh practice, she was, for example, able to "detach from a self that constituted itself through motherhood."

Emiko's younger son, Yoshi, age thirty-two, had severe asthma as a child and was allergic to all foods containing wheat and eggs. When he was young, this isolated him from his classmates. He was the only child who could not eat the school lunch and had to take his own lunchbox of millet balls. To make matters more difficult, he often suffered from severe asthmatic attacks in the middle of the night, and Emiko and her husband, Tatsuya, had to rush him to the hospital in an ambulance. Each time he had an attack, the doctor criticized Emiko for failing to preempt the attack and laid the responsibility on her.

Through learning to develop stillness in her Noh practice, Emiko claimed, she was able to let go of the guilt she had internalized over her son's health and his poor adjustment to society. At thirty-two, he had no gainful employment, and he had dropped out of a school that trains nursing care workers. Emiko attributed his inability to find meaningful work to his precarious health. Her husband sometimes criticized her for not raising their son to be a "normal" person who would fit more easily into society. But in her practiced state of *mushin,* Emiko was able to separate herself from that blame and see the situation differently.

Emiko claimed that cultivating states of *mushin* through her Noh practice facilitated a conversion in her mode of interacting with her husband that allowed her to engage with him in new ways. Emiko notes, "These days, when my husband looks to me to solve our son's problem, I tell him our son is no longer a child. He will need to find his own way. Until I began Noh, I feel I had no capacity to speak out in this way." Emiko felt compassion for her son and this involved acknowledging that he would need to create his own life on his own terms.

Other women I met in the Sumire Kai who were mothers echoed these sentiments. They described situations when their children began to diverge from parental expectations, for instance, by failing their university exams, or by refusing to take on a career path their parents had deemed worthy. Then, through their training, the women realized how deeply identified they were with their children's achievements and that they needed to let go. They were able to take on a philosophical acceptance of their children's separateness from themselves. This nonattachment, in turn, was an important shift for both themselves and their children. In effect, the mothers directed their interest into their own passions rather than monitoring their children's lives. As a son of another Noh practitioner said to me, "People who don't have this kind of activity become very dependent on their kids. In Japan, within families, parents depend on their kids. I'm glad my mother is directing her energy toward Noh. She's very positive and proactive in her approach to life, because of Noh."

True Self

Nishida Kitaro, a Zen philosopher, articulates a notion of no-self that helps to draw out the subtleties of what Csikszentmihalyi and Emiko mean by the emergence of a state of flow and *mushin*. Although Nishida's teachings have come under understandable attack because of his support of militarism in Japan in the 1930s and 1940s, I introduce his ideas to explore the distinctions between an everyday egoistic self and a true self.

The everyday egoistic self is not given in experience but is an abstract self that *seems* to humans to be utterly concrete and real. This self distances the individual from the reality of pure experience or their true self. In order to get to the true self, a person must move beneath the surface noise of ordinary consciousness to a place of pure awareness. To facilitate this process, one can engage in disciplined practice in many body-based arts: Zen seated meditation or walking meditation; a martial art such as *aikido*, *karate*, or *kendo*; or the traditional arts of the tea ceremony, Noh dance, or calligraphy. By stilling the ordinary mind and becoming aware of the quiet stillness of the moment, the true self that resides beneath the chatter of ordinary consciousness surfaces (Nishida in Carter 2001, 149). The true self is without exclusions and is infinite. It is different and the same, here and there. The true self has always been there. It exists in the place "beyond the dualistic bifurcation" that operates "in the field of our everyday experience" (Carter 2001, 173). This transformed state of awareness is akin to what Yuasa Yasuo calls "no-mindedness."

Relationship to Noh Training

Noh training facilitates this process of moving out of an ego-based self for Emiko because it trained her to feel into her dancing body. Whenever she was firmly present to her own sensory experience of the dance, her mind became more quiet. A sense of stillness prevailed. The mind that was judging and analyzing everyday life became more still. The self-consciousness associated with her everyday self also subsided. These experiences created a growing sensory awareness of a state of being where she was alive and present but not seeking to shore up an egoic self. She was instead open to new experiences and to the flow of life.

Emiko's capacity to let go of an egoic self could not have taken place in a vacuum. It was possible because it was supported and reinforced in the pedagogical relationship of the Sumire Kai. The Noh training center was a facilitating environment (Winnicott 1990) where loss of everyday identities was possible.

Emiko claimed that her experience of taking up Noh enabled her to create other opportunities in later life. She created an independent lifeworld distinct from her life as a mother and was able to experience this state of openness. As an example, she described traveling in a group of sixteen women to Italy on a vacation led by two Catholic nuns. Emiko spoke animatedly about her trip. "After all," she exclaimed, "it is about *jibun* (self)." Her eyes danced as she said this, and she repeated this assertion several times during the course of our lunch, as if *jibun* was the genie of her newfound energy.

> I am happy I was able to accept this opportunity, that I was able to know that this opportunity was important. In the past, I've been on international trips with my husband or my family, but I would often do a lot of planning and organizing before the journey. By the time I arrived at the destination, I often had a physical breakdown and lay in bed for days. The most amazing thing, though, was that on this trip, I didn't get sick, not even once.

This particular encounter with Emiko was noteworthy in that she invoked the word *jibun* several times. She mentioned that had she not accepted the opportunity to embark on this trip, she might have "fallen apart." She depicted herself in a way that suggested she was often on the brink of dissolution, and of going under a wave that threatened to overwhelm her.

The bodily manifestation of being overwhelmed in the past was one of having a physical breakdown at her destination.

She mentioned that she had been on international trips with her family in the past. She would go to great lengths to ensure that every part of the itinerary was looked after and that the activities would suit her husband's and sons' preferences. She rarely planned anything on these trips that fitted with her own interests, assuming that such sacrifice was part of being a competent mother. When her husband and children did not enjoy these trips or found something wanting, she recalled feeling resentful and unappreciated.

During this trip to Italy, Emiko enjoyed the company of women, many of whom she had not known prior to leaving for Italy. She and the women visited southern Tuscany and stayed in an old convent for a few days. The women cooked together and took walks in the olive groves. They enjoyed preparing food that drew out the fresh flavors of the local produce: zucchini flowers, red peppers, and eggplant. At night, they went to concerts in the local churches and mingled with the townspeople. She claimed that it was in these moments that she began to notice the experience of the same state of *mushin* that she had experienced in Noh practice. It happened when she ate something that tasted delicious, or when she was cooking with the other women. In those moments, she felt fully alive and invigorated, yet calm. This self is open to new experiences and to the flow of life. It is different from the self that seeks to control outcomes or to enact a particular agenda. It is agentival in one crucial sense in that it makes a conscious decision to live in the moment and to remain present.

Emiko explained to me that she realized that, before, she had tried to be a "perfect" mother and wife who did the right thing by her children and husband. The travel planning she did arose from her own expectations and definitions of a good mother and wife. In later life, she decided to make time to enjoy herself. Emiko's decision to travel to Italy alone without her family was an assertion of her autonomy and her independence. It can be seen as an occasion for a woman like her to say this is the time for me and my enjoyment.

It is important to distinguish between the self that exists in the state of selflessness (the Japanese phrase "sacrifice the self" [*jibun o gisei ni suru*] is another equivalent of selflessness) and the self, *jibun,* that Emiko talks about. This state of selflessness, manifested in wanting to be a perfect mother is actually the location of the egoic self; it is in fact a far cry from being "selfless." Within the ethic of selflessness is a seldom-recognized internal contradiction. It is still ego-based. It needs thus also to be distinguished from the state of no-self. The self that Emiko invoked with such enthusiasm is a different type of self.

Ultimately, in fact, Emiko has two senses of self, and her story has three types overall: a before, egoic self; a nothingness arising from disciplined practice of *mushin*; and an after, more expanded sense of self that comes from the growth of an awareness of the pretensions of the before egoic self. She now has a sense of nothingness, of the true deeper self that is not exclusive or identifiable. She also has a more assertive sense of self.

Learn with Your Body

An experience I had during Noh training points to another associated phenomenon: the loss of everyday identity. One year into my participation in the Noh group, Tsurumi Sensei led me through the song *Hagoromo,* line by line, asking me to repeat after her. Raising one of her fans in the air, she drew a gradated line as she moved the fan across her chest, leading my voice along with it, up, up, then down, then up, and up and up, then down. For a second time, she took me through the play, line by line, getting me to repeat after her, then in the third round getting me to sing the lines by myself. The segment I was learning was only three pages long, but it felt like it had no bounds.

> *Namu kimyô ga tenshi*
> *Onjidai seishi*
> (Hail to thee, Seishi,
> oh thou True Ground of the Moon, daughter of
>   Heaven!)
> *Azuma asobi no mai no kyoku*
> (A dance, then, from the East Country Pleasures.)

My body was shaking and I was pouring out sweat. I indicated to Sensei that I felt overwhelmed and would like to pause the session, but Sensei simply continued. She said, "Look at my mouth. Look at my mouth and learn with your body, Moore-san."

I could feel a certain kind of self-consciousness bobbing around me for a while, knowing that I was with others in the room who were witnessing the molding of rawness: the unshaped voice, the unshaped person trying to incorporate a rhythm and a meter into her being, a way of enunciating and articulating the vowel sounds through the melody. I felt reduced to a mass of humility and effort.

After the session ended and I moved aside for the next student, I remembered something another student, Hiromi, had said about the benefits of practice. "In front of Tsurumi we are all the same. We are made to shed whatever identity we come in with." In her case, it was school principal. My own experience in front of Tsurumi felt even more extreme that day—perhaps, because I was in it. It was not simply a loss of public identity, but a shedding of all: my thoughts, my world, even my pride. This form of training does not always happen because the teaching is often interspersed with lengthy conversations where the teacher talks about herself. But when it happens, the impact is large, like an enormous gust of wind that shakes one to the bone. On one level the experience felt a bit like a confrontation—one that reduced me to a mass of humility and effort—but I also found it extremely refreshing. I could set aside the identities that I had carried into the classroom with me, among them the doctoral candidate from Harvard University, the Australian anthropologist, the woman whose grandmother had given her a shoulder drum. I could put all of those aside and immerse myself in the process of training and learning Noh chanting. I could be in the present. I enjoyed the vocal training in particular and came out of the Noh sessions with an awareness that my self-identity, which was intimately wrapped up with my pride in my ability to maintain self-composure, could slip away. With Sensei's encouragement, I allowed that attachment to self to unravel in class. A new self could be born.

Thus, we see that multiple transitions in the very nature of the self are possible among Noh practitioners. A final set of insights and discoveries relate to the practice of Noh into later life. What are the benefits of practicing Noh into old age?

The Value of Noh in Later Life

Megumi, who is in her seventies, has been doing Noh for forty years. She is one of the designated successors of Tsurumi Sensei's group, in the southern city of Miyazaki. She observes:

> After I became immersed in Noh, I realized that the real instinct of humans is to move to rhythm. I found Noh enjoyable because it allowed me to move with this rhythm. A lot of people stop Noh before they experience this, or they think they won't be able to

enjoy it. For me, it brings so much joy. Once people feel the joys of this rhythm, they will keep on going.

She says, in reference to Noh's suitability for older persons:

> Noh is an activity we can continue to do when we are old. There aren't many things you can continue to do no matter one's age. Even as one's physical mobility deteriorates, one can continue to enjoy Noh. It stimulates the core central muscles of my body. The deep breathing involved in singing is very good for health as well. Noh is very relevant to ordinary life. The body learns the joy of moving (*Karada o ugokasukoto no yorokobi o karada ga shiru*). It teaches one the joys of using one's body. So to me, Noh is most useful. Its benefits can be translated into the rest of our lives.

Her mother, Igarashi Yoko, who is in her nineties, is also a member of the Sumire Kai Noh group. Yoko used to lead a volunteer group for many years. She began Noh at age fifty-five and has been learning Noh for nearly forty years. When I meet her, she says:

> As I grow older, I begin to think a lot about not being a bother to other people. Before, I was in the position of helping other people. Now, as I grow older, I have to find ways to make sure I won't be a burden on others and end up being in a situation where I need to be helped. I see Noh as very important and in a new way to before. I live on my own right now. Using my voice is very important. I have daughters I can chat with, but I spend a lot of time on my own and it's very important to use my voice and chant Noh plays.

Yoko has begun to lose her physical mobility and can no longer perform dances, but she continues to chant. When I visited her last in hospital, she had her Noh songbooks with her. Speaking of her days in the hospital, she says, "It was cold last week, and I asked my daughter to bring me a cardigan. The one she brought was my 'going out' cardigan, which I am saving for my Noh classes. I asked her to put it away and bring me cardigans which are more for everyday wear. I will get dressed in that cardigan and go to class after I recover and leave the hospital. Because I am in and out of hospital, it has become a bit hard to perform in recitals. But I still have a wish to perform *utai* and to bring inspiration and move others."

When asked what else gives her enjoyment, Yoko states:

> At home, I tend to my gardens. Looking after my vegetables keeps me busy. When it becomes a bit warmer, I'm going to plant some new seeds. I really enjoy watching my plants grow. That is a big source of enjoyment for me.

Yoko says she is glad her daughter is the designated successor of Tsurumi Sensei's Miyazaki group. She expresses concern about the future longevity of Noh, and speaks about her grandchildren:

> I want my grandchildren to learn Noh chanting but they haven't taken up *keikogoto*. . . . With the economy being the way it is, it is difficult for younger generations to pay for *keiko*. The economy is becoming worse, and the younger generations don't have that kind of money. I think the numbers of people who can do Noh chanting and dance are becoming increasingly limited across the generations.

Succession

One day Tsurumi Sensei revealed more about what she perceived to be the value of Noh in later life when she discussed the topic of succession. She saw Noh as a vehicle for creating self-reliance in old age. She explained she was having trouble persuading one of her more promising students, Haruko, to become the designated successor of her Sumire Kai group in Fuji-Yoshida in Yamanashi Prefecture. She told me, "I want Haruko-san to reduce the number of volunteer activities she is involved in and devote more of her life to Noh." Haruko was involved in several other activities: she worked as a mediator for the local divorce courts and helped a volunteer organization that raised funds to support development projects in the developing world. But these, Sensei said, would have to take second and third priority.

Tsurumi Sensei's words seem at first self-serving and intended to get Haruko to devote more energy to advance Noh at the expense of other causes. Moreover, at first glance, her involvement in these volunteer organizations seemed similar to her participation in a learning group such as the Sumire Kai. Both fit the definition of social participation (*shakai sanka*) articulated by local governments as a way for senior citizens age sixty and above to remain active members of society. While learning activities may be more mentally taxing, volunteer activities also fit the parameters of active social participation.

I spoke in Haruko's defense, saying that Haruko was very concerned about other people's welfare and sought to make a contribution to the lives of people in more difficult circumstances than herself. The volunteer organization she worked for had raised about US$10,000 to send to the Philippines and Cambodia. Tsurumi Sensei continued, "It's not good to be doing all that volunteering and finally having to be helped by volunteers oneself when one is old. I want her to cultivate her *gei* and gain her *shokutaku* license so that she can teach students one day. Look at me, I'm now over eighty years old, and I am physically very well. I continue to lead an active life as a teacher of Noh. I have students calling me from all over Japan."

Sustained involvement in Noh can be a mode for older persons to maintain their independence in later life. In contemporary Japan, a guiding motif of much social policy language is the virtue of senior citizens remaining healthy and independent in old age. As Long (2012) states, older persons resist dependency.

I asked Haruko how she felt about succession, and she said: "The weight of Sensei's expectations is very large [laughs]." She continued,

> Sensei demands a lot of my time. Sensei is intent on training me. I have had my moments of wanting to escape her! At times, I find the requirement that I dedicate a portion of each week to Noh to be quite onerous. But something changed the year that I performed the play *Tōboku.*
>
> What impressed me was how conscientiously the young Noh performers were seeking to transmit theses rules to us amateurs. When I performed *Tōboku*, the number of rules that govern the performing of Noh struck me: for example, there is a strict set of rules involved in the order in which we put on the costumes.
>
> These young performers are keeping the tradition alive through teaching. It is through their efforts as teachers of the amateurs who perform with them that the young actors are developing their own knowledge and expertise. By participating in this process, my appreciation of my involvement in Noh expanded.

I saw it not just as my own leisure activity but as a living tradition. The role of the amateur is to be involved in the professionals' own professionalization, and through this process—of being a vehicle of listening and embodying these teachings—to sustain Noh for generations.

Referring to the future of her Noh practice, Haruko says, "Noh is likely to become a bigger part of my life once I take over from Sensei and lead the Yamanashi Noh group. The weight

Figure 4.1. Performance of *Tōboku*. Photograph courtesy of Kobayashi Kan.

of Sensei's pressure is very large [laughs again]. But I now see that this heritage stays alive because amateurs participate in it. I want to continue my volunteering activities as well however." Here, we see that Haruko is involved in multiple activities in her later life, of which Noh is simply one. She was somewhat uncertain about the level of commitment that Tsurumi Sensei required of her but her resolve has strengthened. Noh will continue to challenge her, and help her grow well into old age as she becomes more of a leader.

Perpetual Striving

Noh will be a part of Sensei's life for as long as she can keep it. There is no retiring for her. When Tsurumi Sensei and I were storing the Noh songbooks away in her bookcase, I surmised that having dedicated sixty years of her life to Noh practice, all she now sought to do was to transmit all she had learned. She replied, "I want to teach people who don't have what I have. Even if it means to empty myself out completely, I am willing to give everything I know." Tsurumi Sensei pondered a moment further. "But you know what, in order to teach people, I need to mature too. After all, in order for there to be a relationship of trust between student and teacher the student has to feel that the teacher is skilled in teaching. Students have to believe in the teacher's skills in order to become good themselves. I feel I still have a lot to do to polish my *gei*. If there ever comes a day when I feel I've reached a state of perfection then clearly, that would be the day when it is *all over.*" Tsurumi Sensei spoke the last two words emphatically. Her tone suggested that even the attitude that one could stop striving was tantamount to instantiating death. This is not a biological death, of course, but Tsurumi Sensei speaks of it as if it might as well be the end of a meaningful existence.

Her philosophy of perpetual striving extends beyond the domain of artistic work to that of being a good elder. The training she offers at the Sumire Kai is a form of discipline, especially for people as they become older. "As one ages, our emotions become blunted. We make less of an effort to get along with others. I know from my own experience that we are not willing to extend ourselves for others in the ways we might have when we were younger and more energetic." In her view, coming to the Sumire Kai helps her students remain "young" because the approach to learning involves being mindful and considerate of other people. She teaches them rules and etiquette on how to comment on the performance of other students, offer praise, and provide feedback in constructive rather than hurtful ways. She reminds her students that the health benefits of Noh chanting and dance extend beyond deep breathing and the building of core strength. "The rituals of learning together, getting along with others, and conversing with different people in the class are very important for sustaining a social self in later life." Without such opportunities to practice social interaction, she thinks that older people are likely to decline more rapidly.

Conclusion

In this chapter, I delved into student testimonials about the experience of learning. In particular, I explored the processes of identity formation and dissolution and the state of no-mind that arise from practicing Noh. These experiential states, in turn, have important benefits on the everyday lives of these amateur women practitioners. Some are about experiencing flow, and some are about Noh as an asset that continues well into old age. Noh undertaken as a lifework of disciplined practice provides strength to older women in the Sumire Kai. In a time of life when loss and change are common, practicing a traditional performing art brings a special kind of reward. The meaningfulness comes from the subtle improvements and refinements in technique that each woman experiences, which serve to affirm the individual's feeling of possibility about their own growth in later life. Sustained involvement in a lifework can be a mode for older persons to maintain their independence in later life. Working with a group, the women are sharing their discoveries with other people. Their involvement in Noh provides them with a sense of purpose, an important basis for social participation, and a sense of participating in a living tradition.

5

——————

Acceptance

This brief chapter is a further reflection on the process of letting go of attachment to egoic self. I explore the theme of acceptance, drawing on a vignette of Yoshiko, who is training to be a nun in western Japan. I argue that an integral aspect of the expansion of self discussed in the previous chapter is the acceptance of otherness of the self.

The vignette that follows of Yoshiko scrubbing the moss from stone statues is a central touchstone for understanding the mystery of peeling away of identity that I have discussed in this book: the meaningfulness of leisure comes from the possibility implied by moments when we do not experience desire or identity and attachment to the egoic self, including attachment to a sense of mastery. It arises when those recede and drift away. It is in these moments that an expanded sense of self is truly possible. And so acceptance of the moments of fallibility that arise in the process of identity formation is also important.

Scrubbing the Moss

Yoshiko has come to the Zen nunnery. She is sixty, a former physicist who worked at a university as an academic researcher, and is now in her second year of training to become a Zen nun at a temple for monastic training (*dôjô*) in western Japan. She arrived at the temple dressed in her Zen garb. Gathered at the temple on this hot August day are the abbess, the chef, Yoshiko, and myself. We are eager to hear how Yoshiko has been faring at the *dôjô*. After lunch, Yoshiko tells us the story of what happened before the annual festival (*jizô bon*) that memorializes the *jizô* statues that protect children, which had been held the previous day at her temple. In preparation for the festival, the head of the temple (*dôchô*) had asked Yoshiko to clean the *jizô* statues. Yoshiko described her experience:

> As I was washing the statues, the *dôchô* came and said to me, "You can simply wash the big ones at the front. There's no need to wash them all." I replied that I would wash all the *jizô*. The *dôchô* simply watched for a few moments, not saying anything, as I scrubbed the stone figures. Then finally, the *dôchô* said, "Do you want me to bring detergent?" With that she went away and returned a short while later with a bottle of yellow detergent. I took the bottle of detergent and squirted it over the statues and proceeded to scrub each one until all the moss had been scrubbed away.

The abbess, who was sitting at the table, leaned forward slightly and said with a tone of alarm, "You washed off all the moss?"

Yoshiko nodded.

The abbess continued, "You know, moss reflects the flow of time. It doesn't grow in a day. That the *jizô* came to be covered in moss shows that they have weathered and been there in the rain and wind for years. To think you just scrubbed off all the moss until the stones were raw. Well, what can I say?"

There was an awkward silence in the room as Yoshiko, the chef, and I sat in silence. It was clear that the abbess was flummoxed by Yoshiko's story. The abbess then began to chuckle. "Indeed that is so Zen," she said. "In Zen they do not teach you directly. They do not say 'do this, do that.' You need to learn to judge for yourself."

Yoshiko hung her head and mumbled, "I am always making mistakes. I have made another mistake." She sat despondently, and then added, "But I wish the head of the temple had told me. Come to think of it, she did tell me to stop! But she didn't tell me what it was that I was doing wrong. I wonder then why she brought the detergent." Yoshiko knitted her forehead in puzzlement.

The abbess said quietly, "She probably brought the detergent to shake you into reflecting on what you were doing."

Yoshiko was chagrined and said again, "Oh why didn't I understand?"

The abbess was silent for a while. Then she started chuckling again. She said, repeatedly, "That's a great story." And as if to herself, chuckling some more, she said, "To think you washed the *jizô* statues with detergent."

Yoshiko put her hand to her head and said, "Why am I so daft?"

Yoshiko claimed to me that she was frustrated because she felt that her many years of training in analysis and argumentation in academe did not serve her well in the *dôjô*. If anything, it put her at a disadvantage compared to other trainees, who were not as mired in an analytical perspective and who seemed more able to listen to the cues from the Zen nun.

On one level, this vignette is about the faux pas that Yoshiko has committed. Rather than be open and responsive to the *dôchô*'s voice that tells her to stop scrubbing, she remains intent on completing a task that she had decided in her own mind is a good idea. In her perception, the moss is simply unwanted detritus or debris. It is something to act upon, remove, so as to return the *jizô* to a state of pure rock. Rather than regard the moss with reverence, as evidence of the passage of time, and the work of the Elements on the exposed rock, it is something to be cleared away.

Although what Yoshiko was doing was not intrinsically absurd, she was doing it thoughtlessly and was unaware of her desires to complete the task of cleaning, which were what was absurd. She was doggedly attached to her own plan to complete the task of cleaning. Presumably, the *dôchô* knew that if Yoshiko became aware of her desires, they would give up their hold on her. Desire is how subjects make and reassure themselves, fix themselves in a world of flux through attachment to a fantasized future. For example, they may treat time—and the difference it brings—as if it does not really happen, as if it does not come between them and their goals, and as if they are masters of their lives and worlds (see Hegel in Kojeve 1969). In her attachment to the idea she had formed in her mind, Yoshiko could no longer hear the words of the *dôchô* nor even pause to reflect on why the *dôchô* may have brought her the detergent to clean stone statues.

At another level, this vignette has a deeper significance. The deeper implication lies in the very fact that Yoshiko is telling it, openly, to the abbess, the chef, and me with an innocence and honesty and undue self-criticism. That is, in telling this story, Yoshiko is not attached to putting on an appearance of competence and proving to the abbess that she is succeeding at the *dôjô,* solving *kôan* well, and sailing smoothly as she should. Neither is she speaking in self-pity in such a way that she seeks sympathy and reassurance from the abbess. She is simply telling what happened.

In her honest telling, what comes through is an acceptance of where she is now. We see here real humility in this acceptance. It is an acceptance of the difference and otherness in the self and the things that Yoshiko may have hoped to grow away from. Mastery lies, then, not in having transcended the egoic self, but in the lack of attachment to it, which translates to her capacity to start afresh. Also, Yoshiko's scrubbing of the moss was not really a mistake if, with awareness, it became the path, the way and the only way for Yoshiko to move forward, given that she cannot undo what she has already done.

Acceptance is a central aspect of maturity. It is the capacity to be with, acknowledge, and observe the state in which one is. It is about compassion for the complex multidimensionality of one's state, including one's limitations, which like the *jizo* statues, can either be cleaned away or let be, moss and all. Some refer to this capacity for acceptance as the expansion of a capacity to tolerate limitations, where tolerate has the nuance of "putting up with" these limitations. A more apt way of referring to this is the capacity to "be with" these limitations. "Being with" something is very subtle. It is about nonattachment. It happens when the attachment to the self has receded. Being with grows with the capacity to let the self slip away.

Conclusion

Contemporary observers of Japanese society remark upon the rapid aging of Japan and what impact the aging of the population will have on Japanese culture. Japan is at the forefront of having to grapple with a rapid rise in the number of senior citizens. Amateur learning of Noh chanting and dance is an important facet of later life learning in Japan today. Governments support senior citizens' involvement in learning activities as a form of social participation and a medium for active aging. There is a boom in elders seeking to learn new things, especially following retirement. Older citizens are staying active, especially against a background of greater policy rhetoric that addresses the need for senior citizens to exercise self-reliance and personal responsibility (Kawano 2010).

Noh learning is a highly productive and useful lens through which to analyze a range of social phenomena in Japan. It shows the quest for creating new lives in retirement, and for creating active aging and meaning in later life. Noh training is one of the large array of learning activities available to older women in contemporary Japan to invigorate their "second lives." Women gather to receive intensive physical and vocal training. By engaging in this training, they catapult themselves into new social networks and a sense of identity based on membership in a world of shared learning. In the Sumire Kai learning site, a sense of camaraderie is fostered by various rituals and practices, regular recitals, and a common repertoire of plays.

Particularly important is the strong pedagogical relationship. These dimensions create a sense of being on a shared path and friendship born through a common pursuit.

Like other forms of leisure and recreation available to older adults in contemporary Japan, Noh training is an embodied practice, which emphasizes the mastery of specific physical moves and vocal expression. What makes Noh distinct from other forms of learning is that its practitioners are primarily members of Japan's middle and upper-middle classes. Noh's historical association with members of Japan's social elite (government leaders, owners of companies, and the nobility) gives it an air of exclusivity that contributes to the perception of Noh as an arcane art. Moreover, in contemporary Japanese society where the middle class has hollowed out due to Japan's long recession, the high fees associated with Noh training signify a certain class distinction for those who can afford it. It would be difficult to make Noh a universal hobby.

In every fieldwork experience, one encounter radically shapes the direction of the research project. In my case, it was my encounter with the teacher of Noh singing and dance, Tsurumi Sensei. As the head teacher of the Sumire Kai, a community of eighty women and men devoted to learning and performing Noh, Tsurumi Sensei was responsible for transmitting the art of Noh to a lay audience.

Tsurumi Sensei's life of cultivation and discipline, forged in her teenage years, becomes legitimation for her to take on a leadership role in old age and lead other older people to learn Noh. Tsurumi Sensei's story is emblematic of women's struggle to contest the narrow sphere of possibilities available to women in postwar Japan. Family and gender relations within the home are major forces that shaped Tsurumi Sensei's subjectivity and identity. Pivotal to her life was the early encounter with Noh taught to her by her maternal uncle, who drilled her in Noh songs in the fields near a rice paddy in southern Japan during

World War II. He was a force that ignited her commitment to Noh training and to the transmission of this art form today. Her uncle's message continues to reverberate through her life and the lives of her students:

> Real cultivation is not about what you acquire and attach to yourself, as an adornment. It is the discipline that you imbue into your body. It is what will make you shine. No matter what strife befalls you, polish your voice and dancing. Chant, Reiko! Chant. This art will create a luster from within that nothing and nobody can take away from you. Your *gei* will shine from within you.

We see this discipline manifesting in her classroom, giving a sense of order and structure to her life and to others.

The Transformative Power of Learning

I have argued that we can approach learning activities as more than a vehicle for establishing social status and respectability, but also as a medium for exploring the development of selves. Ethnographic research on women in the Sumire Kai leads me to take issue with scholarly analyses of cultural pursuits that primarily interpret these acts as modes of establishing social distinction. A chief example of this genre of work is Pierre Bourdieu's (1984) study of taste and distinction. Unrelenting in his commitment to exposing the reproduction of social inequality and barriers to social mobility, Bourdieu launched an analysis of cultural pursuits of the French middle class within this frame, as a technology for preserving social stratification. Bourdieu incisively illuminated the ways in which consumption of leisure and art operates as a means to uphold class differences. While fully respecting Bourdieu's trenchant analysis, I nonetheless argue that this single-minded focus on analyzing consumption in this mode, as a tool for establishing social distinction and reproducing social inequality, prevents us from gaining other important analytical insights into leisure practices.

Multiple factors operate in the pursuit of learning by women in Japan beyond establishing social distinction. They include the quest for new social relations outside of the family network, the desire for physical mastery, and the quest for growth in later life, a form of growth made possible by a strict but supportive relationship between pedagogue and student. Also important is the quest for *mushin*. *Mushin* is a state of present awareness. It is a relaxed state of mind, in which people are conscious of their experience, including sensations, breathing, and their surroundings, all with an attitude of acceptance. This does not imply passivity or lack of emotion. A sense of nothingness allows each new experience to be felt fully, without the controlling mind interfering in the experience. It involves a state of heightened awareness of being, releasing the grip of the everyday self, and breaking the chain of reactivity.

Similar to Wearing (1998), I have argued that we can conceptualize leisure in terms of a social space that allows for modes of being that are different from those of the everyday constraints of human life. Leisure is both a space of resistance to male domination and a space for women's own enlargement or growth. Moreover, inherent in this notion of space is process, where selves are generated relationally through acts such as speaking, performing, and communicating. Writing of Pacific Islander women, Wearing states that these women create spaces of pleasure by talking, sharing poetry, and humor. These spaces restore to them a sense of self-worth and community. Similar observations can be made about women in the Sumire Kai.

My aim in this ethnography has been to offer insight into body-based learning. Practitioners gain meaning by participating in and experiencing the ongoing life of a performing tradition through embodying it and experiencing its effects on their lives, rather than simply valuing it as a marker of their social identity. When they are embodying tradition, they are experiencing what Csikszentmihalyi (1991) calls flow. There is a sensation of deep, focused involvement in the activity. There is sometimes an alteration in their sense of time. Importantly, there is disappearance of consciousness of everyday self. In flow, the sense of time is suspended. They are also in what Eliade calls "eternal" time (1971[1954], 149). In eternal time, the distinction between past and present is suspended. As a consequence, the referential quality of tradition, as something that represents the past and is valuable because it points to the past, recedes in importance. This focus on embodiment has implications for how we understand the value of tradition in everyday life. Tradition is alive through the experience of participation in the rite. This experience is what gives tradition its immediacy, its tangibility, and its relevance to those who practice it.

Another aim in this ethnography has been to examine how the process of learning and experiencing Noh intertwines with the everyday identities of women practitioners, in particular those of retiree and mother. Many women begin Noh in midlife, from their late fifties, when they are anticipating retiring from their primary careers and are looking to develop their "second lives" after retirement. The rigors of training, the close relationship that students form with the teacher, and the friendships women develop through the Noh practice are important for these women's personal development. Motherhood is often associated with states of self-sacrifice, selflessness, and compliance with familial expectations, and is made central to a mature woman's identity. Many have had limited opportunities for public recognition of their personal efforts, and operated with gender norms that encouraged them to support family members rather than seek that support themselves. Scholars of Japanese motherhood more generally have pointed out that women's ongoing collaboration with children is seen as a praiseworthy sign of devotion and self-sacrifice (Borovoy 2005). Childhood dependency is seen to lay the foundation for children's future success and social engagement. Yet, this cultural expectation is burdensome, for both children and mothers. I have discussed how Noh practice enables women to address some of the challenges associated with this cultural expectation of the selfless mother and create a new life. Through Noh training, women can develop an independent lifeworld, distinct from their familial lives, and in the process develop distance from their identities as mothers.

These performing arts communities centering on learning and transmission of embodied knowledge create vitality and well-being. In the process women put their own stamp on these traditions, and make them their own. They imbue their own spirit into these forms, thereby giving them new meaning.

Many amateur practitioners share the concerns of the Japan Arts Council to sustain the traditional performing arts. The Japanese government has sought to protect the traditional performing arts by designating highly gifted practitioners as Important Intangible Cultural Properties. This designation affords a degree of state protection to Noh as well as to its performers. Tsurumi Sensei and the amateurs who are featured in this ethnography participate in Noh with the desire to sustain this art form. They come to see it as more than their own leisure activity and rather from the point of view of participants in sustaining a living tradition. The role of the amateur is to be involved in the professionals' own professionalization, and through this process—of being a vehicle for listening and embodying these teachings—to sustain Noh for generations. Many are concerned about the waning of this classical theatre. As amateurs, Tsurumi Sensei's students do not have official responsibility to ensure that Noh continues into the future, but many want Noh to thrive.

While the high costs of learning Noh make it suitable for only a limited sector of the Japanese population, the expansion of the aging population in Japan is an opportunity for more Japanese to explore the benefits of Noh, and for Noh performers to teach their art to larger numbers of older practitioners. The rituals of Noh learning, in fact, have much to contribute toward sustaining well-being. The rigors of training, the close relationship students form with the teacher, and the friendships women develop through the Noh practice are important. The Noh class offers a space for older persons to share their ongoing discoveries and development. This network is important to their well-being. The health benefits associated with Noh, such as the emphasis on deep breathing and increase in physical stability and powers of concentration, are also worth noting. Given the future expansion in the numbers of senior citizens in Japan, there is ample room for this traditional performing art to be adopted as an art form that engenders health and well-being among older persons.

Glossary of Noh Terms

Deshi	弟子	apprentice
Fushi	節	melody
Gei	芸	art
Iemoto	家元	hereditary head of Noh school
Hayashi	囃子	instruments of the Noh theater (flute, hip drum, shoulder drum, and stick drum)
Kai	会	group
Keiko	稽古	training
Kotsuzumi	小鼓	shoulder drum
Shimai	仕舞	Noh dance
Shirôto	素人	amateur
Suri-ashi	すり足	Noh gliding steps
Utai	謡	Noh chanting

Works Cited

Abelmann, N. 1997. Narrating selfhood and personality in South Korea: Women and social mobility. *American Ethnologist* 24, no. 4: 786–812.

Ambaras, D. 1998. Social knowledge: Cultural capital and the new middle class in Japan, 1895–1912. *Journal of Japanese Studies* 24, no. 1: 1–33.

Aoki, R. 2012. The construction of Japanese Noh theatre as a masculine art: An analysis of its traditional and modern discourses. Paper presented at the Annual Meeting of the Asian Studies Association, Toronto, Canada, March 17, 2012.

Barthes, R. 1984. *Camera Lucida.* London: Flamingo.

Bestor, T. C. 2003. "Inquisitive observation: Following networks in urban fieldwork." In *Doing fieldwork in Japan,* ed T. C. Bestor, P. Steinhoff, and V. L. Bestor. Honolulu: University of Hawaii Press.

———. 2004. *Tsukiji: The fish market at the center of the world.* Berkeley, Los Angeles, London: University of California Press.

Bethe, M., and K. Brazell. 1982. *Dance in the Noh theater.* Ithaca: China-Japan Program, Cornell University.

Borovoy, A. 2005. *The too-good wife: Alcohol, codependency, and the politics of nurturance in postwar Japan.* Berkeley, California: University of California Press.

Bourdieu, P. 1984. *Distinction: A social critique of the judgment of taste.* London: Routledge and Kegan Paul.

Brazell, K. 1998. Elements of performance. In *Traditional Japanese theatre: An anthology of plays,* ed. K. Brazell, 115–25. New York: Columbia University Press.

Brown, S. T. 2001. *Theatricalities of power: The cultural politics of Noh.* Stanford: Stanford University Press.

Butler, J. 1990. *Gender trouble: Feminism and the subversion of identity.* London: Psychology Press.

Cabinet Office. 2011. *White paper on the aging society.* (*Kôresiha shakai hakusho*). Tokyo: Government Publishing Bureau.

Campbell, J. C. 1992. *How policies change: The Japanese government and the aging society.* Princeton: Princeton University Press.

Carter, R. E. 2001. *Encounter with enlightenment: A study of Japanese ethics.* Albany: State University of New York Press.

Columbia Music Entertainment. 2002. *Yokyoku* (Noh song). Online. Available: http://jtrad.columbia.jp/eng/n_yokyoku.html; accessed Aug. 12, 2013.

Creighton, M. 2001. Spinning silk, weaving selves: Nostalgia, gender, and identity in Japanese craft vacations. *Japanese Studies* 21, no. 1: 5–29.

Csikszenthmiyalyi, M. 1991. *Flow: The psychology of optimal experience.* New York: Harper Perennial.

de Certeau, M. 1984. *The practice of everyday life.* Trans. S. Rendall. Berkeley: University of California Press.

De Vos, G. A. and H. Wagatsuma. 1984. *Heritage of endurance: Family patterns and delinquency formation in urban Japan.* Berkeley: University of California Press.

Desjarlais, R. 1996. The office of reason: On the politics of language and agency in a shelter for the homeless mentally ill. *American Ethnologist* 23, no. 4: 880–900.

Doi, T. 1977. *Amae no Kōzō.* (*The anatomy of dependence*). Tokyo and New York: Kodansha International.

Durkheim, E. and K. Fields. 1995. *The elementary forms of religious life.* Translated by Karen Fields. New York: The Free Press.

Ebron, P. A. 2002. *Performing Africa.* Princeton: Princeton University Press.

Ejima, Ihei. 1967. "Sengo no Tachiagari [A new start after the war]." *Nôgaku Shichô* 40: 5–8.

Eliade, M. 1971 [1954]. *The myth of the eternal return, or Cosmos and history.* Princeton: Princeton University Press.

Fraleigh, S. 2000. Consciousness matters. *Dance Research Journal* 32, no. 1: 54–62.

Fuess, H. 2004. *Divorce in Japan: Family, gender, and the state, 1600–2000*. Studies of the East Asian Institute. Stanford: Stanford University Press.

———. 2005. Men's place in the women's kingdom: New middle-class fatherhood in Taisho Japan. In *Public spheres, private lives in modern Japan, 1600–1950: Essays in honor of Albert M. Craig*, ed. G. L. Bernstein, A. Gordon, and K. Wildman Nakai. Cambridge: Harvard University Asia Center. Distributed by Harvard University Press.

Game, A., and A. Metcalfe. 2008. Potential space and love. *Emotion, Space and Society* 1, no. 1: 18–21.

Geilhorn, B. 2008. Between self-empowerment and discrimination: Women in Noh today. In *Noh theatre transversal*, ed. S. Scholz-Cionca and C. Balme, 106–22. Munich: Ludicium Verlag.

Government Statistics Bureau. 2006. Vital statistics. http://www.stat. go.jp/data/nihon/02.htm. Accessed March 24, 2007.

Horikami, K., K. Yasuharu, M. Tadashi, and T. Kunito. 2010. Nôkai tenbô; Yôkyoku jinkô no suitai o megutte. (A view of the Noh world: The decline in population of Noh chanting enthusiasts). *Nôgaku Journal* 60: 18–21.

Ishii, K., and N. Jarkey. 2002. The housewife is born: The establishment of the notion and identity of the *Shufu* in modern Japan. *Japanese Studies* 22, no. 1: 35–52.

Japan Statistics Bureau. Family Income and Expenditure Survey. Online. Available: http://www.stat.go.jp/english/data/kakei/ct2010.htm; accessed Aug. 12, 2013.

Kadono, H. 2000. *Rôshin o suteraremasuka? (Can you abandon your older relatives?)* Tokyo: Shufu no Tomosha, Kodansha Bunko.

Kamishima, J. 1964. *Nihonjin no kekkon kan*. Tokyo: Kawade Shobo.

Kanamori, A. 1994. *Onnaryû tanjô: Nôgakushi Tsumura Kimiko no shôgai. (The birth of female Noh: The biography of Noh performer Tsumura Kimiko)*.Tokyo: Hosei Daigaku Shuppankyoku.

Kato, E. 2002. "Art" for men, "manners" for women: How women transformed the tea ceremony in modern Japan. In *Women as sites of culture: Women's roles in cultural formation from the*

Renaissance to the twentieth century, ed. S. Shifrin. Hampshire, UK: Ashgate.

———. 2004. *The tea ceremony and women's empowerment in modern Japan.* London and New York: RoutledgeCurzon.

Kawano, S. 2010. *Nature's embrace: Japan's aging urbanites and new death rites.* Honolulu: University of Hawaii Press.

Keene, D., and R. Tyler. 1970. *Twenty plays of the Nō theatre.* New York: Columbia University Press.

Klein, S. B. 1991. When the moon strikes the bell: Desire and enlightenment in the Noh play *Dōjōji. Journal of Japanese Studies* 17, no. 2: 291–322.

Kleinman, A. 1988. *The illness narratives: Suffering, healing, and the human condition.* New York: Basic Books.

Koike, S. 2003. *Kôreika shakai to shôgai gakushû* [The Aging Society and Lifelong Learning]. In *Shôgai gakushû o torimaku shakai kankyô* [Social issues surrounding lifelong learning], ed. H. Sasaki. Tokyo: Gakubunsha.

Kojeve, A. 1969. *Introduction to the reading of Hegel.* New York: Basic Books.

Kondo, D. 1990. *Crafting selves: Power, gender, and discourses of identity in a Japanese workplace.* Chicago: University of Chicago Press.

Konparu, K. 1983. *The Noh theater: Principles and perspectives.* 1st ed. New York: Weatherhill/Tankosha.

Lave, J., and E. Wenger. 1992. *Situated learning: Legitimate peripheral participation.* Cambridge and New York: Cambridge University Press.

Lebra, T. S. 1993. *Above the clouds: Status culture of the modern Japanese nobility.* Berkeley: University of California Press.

Long, S. O. 2012. Bodies, technologies, and aging in Japan: Thinking about old people and their silver products. *Journal of Cross-Cultural Gerontology* 27: 119–37.

Matsumoto, Y. 2011. Introduction. In *Faces of aging: The lived experiences of the older persons in Japan,* ed. Y. Matsumoto, 1–16. Stanford: Stanford University Press.

Merleau-Ponty, M. 1962. *Phenomenology of perception,* London: Routledge.

Metcalfe, A., and A. Game. 2007. Becoming who you are: The time of education. *Time and Society* 16, no. 1: 43–59.

Miyanishi, N. 2005. *Josei nôgakushi to futatsu no kabe: Nôgaku kyôkai to nihon nôgaku kyôkai nyûkai.* (A study of two barriers against female Noh professionals). *Nihon University Graduate School of Social and Cultural Studies Bulletin* 6: 86–97.

Moore, K. 2012. Singing in the workplace: Salarymen and the amateur Noh theatre. *Asian Theatre Journal* 29, no. 1: 164–82.

Mori, B. L. R. 1991. The tea ceremony: A transformed Japanese ritual. *Gender and Society* 5, no. 1: 86–100.

Nishiyama, M. 1982. *Iemotosei no tenkai* [Development of the Iemoto System]. Tokyo: Yoshikawa Kôbunkan.

Nohgaku Performers' Association (*Nohgaku Kyôkai*). Membership. Online. Available: http://www.nohgaku.or.jp/members; accessed Aug. 12, 2013.

Ogamo, R. T. 2002–03. Women in Noh today. In *Theater East and West Revisited,* ed. C. Davis. Special Issue of *Mime Journal*: 67–80.

———. (Noh practitioner of the Kongo School). Personal Interview, Feb. 17, 2011.

Ogawa, A. 2009. Japan's New Lifelong Learning Policy: Exploring Lessons from the European Knowledge Economy. *International Journal of Lifelong Education* 28, no. 5: 601–14.

Okamoto, A. 2008. The actor's body in Nô and contemporary theatre: On the work of Ren'niku Kôbô. In *Noh theatre transversal,* ed. S. Scholz-Cionca and C. Balme, 106–22. Munich: Ludicium Verlag.

Okumoto, K. 1994. *Shôgai gakushû seisaku.* [Lifelong learning policy]. Tokyo: Zen Nihon Kyôiku Rengô Kai.

Owen, L. 2008. *Her blood is gold: Awakening to the wisdom of menstruation.* Dorset, UK: Archive Publishing.

Plath, D. W. 1980. *Long engagements, Maturity in modern Japan.* Stanford: Stanford University Press.

Rath, E. 2001. Challenging the old men: A brief history of women in Noh theater. *Women and Performance: a Journal of Feminist Theory* 12. *Special Issue: Performing Japanese Women,* ed. S. T. Brown and S. Jensen: 97–111.

———. 2004. *The ethos of Noh: Actors and their art.* Cambridge and London: Harvard University Asia Center. Distributed by Harvard University Press.

Rohlen, T. P. 1974. *For harmony and strength: Japanese white-collar organization in anthropological perspective.* Berkeley: University of California Press.

Shiraishi, Y. 1998. *Alternative approaches to financing lifelong learning.* Geneva: OECD.

Shiroma, S., and Y. Moro. 2007. An analysis of the learning process for a Noh dance: Social construction of the novice's motor skills within club activities. *Tsukuba Psychological Research* 33: 9–28.

Singleton, J. C. 1998. Introduction. In *Learning in likely places: Varieties of apprenticeship in Japan,* ed. J. C. Singleton. Cambridge and New York: Cambridge University Press.

Stebbins, R. 2006. *Serious leisure: A perspective for our time.* New Brunswick, NJ: Transaction Publishers.

Takahashi, K., M. Tokoro, and H. Giyoo. 2011. Successful aging through participation in social activities among senior citizens: Becoming photographers. In *Faces of aging: The lived experiences of the older persons in Japan,* ed. Y. Matsumoto, 17–35. Stanford: Stanford University Press.

Terasaki, E. 2002. *Figures of desire: Wordplay, spirit possession, fantasy, madness, and mourning in Japanese Noh plays.* Ann Arbor: Center for Japanese Studies, University of Michigan.

Traphagan, J. W. 2000. *Taming oblivion: Aging bodies and the fear of senility in Japan.* Albany: State University of New York Press.

———. 2006. Being a good *rôjin*: Senility, power, and self-actualization in Japan. In *Thinking about dementia: Culture, loss, and the anthropology of senility,* ed. A. Leibing and L. Cohen. New Brunswick, NJ: Rutgers University Press.

Ueno, C. 2007. *Ohitorisama no rōgo.* (*Old age for the single elder*). Tokyo: Hōken.

Uno, K. 1998. The death of good wife, wife mother? In *Dimensions of contemporary Japan: A collection of essays,* ed. E. Beauchamp, New York and London: Garland Publishing.

Uzawa, Hisa. 2008. Reflections on performing for the international *nô* symposium. In *Noh theatre transversal,* ed Stanca Scholz-Cionca and Christopher Balme, 106–22. Munich: Ludicium Verlag.

Vogel, E. 1973, Kinship structure, migration to the city, and modernization. In *Aspects of social change in modern Japan,* ed. R. P. Dore. Princeton: Princeton University Press.

Vogel, S. 1978. Professional housewife: The career of urban middle class Japanese women. In *Women and women's issues in post World War II Japan,* ed. E. Beauchamp. Tokyo and London: Garland Publishing.

Wacquant, L. 1995. The pugilistic point of view: How boxers think and feel about their trade. *Theory and Society* 24, no. 4: 489–535.

Wakita, H. 2005. *Nôgaku no naka no Onna tachi.* (*Women in the Noh theater*). Tokyo: Seikôsha.

Wearing, B. 1998. *Leisure and feminist theory.* London: Sage Publications.

Winnicott, D.W. 1990. The capacity to be alone. In *The maturational processes and the facilitating environment.* London: Karnac Books.

———. 1991. *Playing and reality.* London: Routledge.

Wulff, H. 1998. *Ballet across borders: Career and culture in the world of dancers.* Oxford: Berg.

Yamanaka, R. 2008. What features distinguish Noh from other performing arts? In *Noh theatre transversal,* ed. S. Scholz-Cionca and C, Balme, 106–22. Munich: Ludicium Verlag.

Yano, K. K. 2004. *Kyôiku sangyô hakusho.* [Education industry white paper.] Tokyo: Yano Keizai Kenkyûjo.

Yasuda, K. 1989. *Masterworks of the Nō theater.* Bloomington: Indiana University Press.

Yuasa, Y. 1993. *The body, self-cultivation, and ki-energy.* Trans. S. Nagatomo and M. S. Hull. Albany: State University of New York Press.

Zeami, M. 1984. *On the art of the Noh drama: The major treatises of Zeami.* Trans. T. J. Rimer and M. Yamazaki. Princeton: Princeton University Press.

Index

www.ingramcontent.com/pod-product-compliance
Lightning Source LLC
Chambersburg PA
CBHW020356270326
41926CB00007B/462